THE RED RIDER

THE OBSIDIAN SPINDLE SAGA

BOOK FOUR

RUSSELL NOHELTY

SPECIAL THANKS

Adriane Ruzak, Amanda Jackson, Angela, Anthony Bachman, Caledonia, Caspar Williams, Celeste and Bryan Cornish, Chad Bowden, Chris Call, Chris Meeson, Christopher C Epping, Christopher Prew, CJ Ives Lopez, Daniel Biittner, Daniel Groves, Dave Baxter, Dave Goldberg, David Chamberlain, David Drummond, David Straube, Desiree Duffy, DJ Inzeo, Ed S, Edward Nycz Jr., Emerson Kasak, Erin Congdon, Gabriella Farmer, Gary Phillips, Hannah Long, Hollie Buchanan II, Jeff Lewis, Jennifer & Charlie Geer, John C. Heller, Johnny Britt, Jon Tugan, Joshua Bowers, Joshua Pantalleresco, Juli, Kimberly Herout, Larry Gilman, Lincoln City Archery, Lisa Homolka, Lisa Lyons, Matthew Johnson, Maxi Organ, Melissa Showers, Michael Kingston, Michael Perler, Mike Jones, Monkey King Comics, Nic Nelson, Nick Smith, Paul Rose Jr., Per Stalby, Rachel Adams, Rhel ná DecVandé, Richard A Williams, Rob MacAndrew, Rowan, S.A. McClure, Salvatore Puma, Scott Kilburn, Stephen Ballentine, Steven "Waffles" Lane, Taiga Char, Talinda Willard (everfai), Victoria Nohelty, and Walter Weiss

The Red Rider
Book 4 of the Obsidian Spindle Saga

By:
Russell Nohelty

Edited by:
Leah Lederman

Proofread by:
Katrina Roets

Cover by:
JV Arts

Formatting by:
Turbo Kitten Industries

CHAPTER 1
RED

The Mountain Realm.

Getting here nearly killed me.

But I arrived, and in one piece.

The army from the Nightmare Realm was formidable and hideous, but they were dumb and easy to outmaneuver on foot, especially if you weren't overburdened with other people. I had abandoned my sand salamander long ago, as the dust and dirt it kicked up gave away my position. The desert was a slog, but once I entered the hilly terrain of the mountains, it was easier to conceal my trail.

Besides, the monsters weren't looking for me, they were looking for a fight. The Golden Sun of Sekhmet's troops waited for them at the border between the Mountain Realm and the lion god's Sandlands.

From the base of Agrona's Mountain, I was sure I could see the fight raging in the distance, but it was impossible. My mind was playing tricks on me. The fighting took place beyond the horizon, two days' journey behind me. Even my perfect eyesight could not make out fifty miles in the distance.

As I took a moment to catch my breath, a hot wind blew past my face. The trees above me quivered, signaling a massive monster making its way through the forest. I rolled behind an exposed rock. The branches above me snapped, and a giant molten foot smashed down onto the ground with a loud crash. Another foot smashed down in front of it slowly, plodding, without any sense of urgency. There was no need to be urgent when every step the lava golem took carried it a hundred yards forward.

Three more steps and the quaking around me stopped; the golem shrank in the distance. I didn't know what kind of beacon called the monsters of the Nightmare Realm to the border of the Sandlands, but every monster I came across was making a beeline for the battlefront. Their singular focus made it easier to avoid them.

I clasped Sekhmet's necklace tightly in my fingers and closed my eyes. She told me the necklace would protect me from the horror of the Nightmare Realm, and so far I had been safe from attack, but I would never know if that was because of my own prowess or because of the charm given to me by the lioness.

"Please, please, please," I mumbled to the charm. "This has to work. Gods of Urgu, protect and guide my steps."

There was a long way to go before my quest was over. I needed to make it over the mountains and into the Land of Oz, and then dive into the water past the Emerald City where Nox made her home under the sea, protected by the vicious mermaids. I once thought that the mermaids were protectors of the Obsidian Spindle, but had come to understand that they served Nox, goddess of the dark. They were guardians of a key that Sekhmet required to end this war between Urgu and the Nightmare Realm.

Nox was also the mother of both Epiales, god of nightmares, and Hypnos, god of dreams and true ruler of the Dream Realm. He had long abandoned us; he hadn't been seen in the Dream Realm in a hundred years. Epiales was taking advantage of that fact. In the Dream God's absence, the god of nightmares worked to take control of Urgu, and everything it touched. Without Hypnos, the only being who had more power than Epiales in the Dream Realm was Nox, and thus it was my quest to find her. I could not fail. If I did, then we would all be doomed.

It would not be easy. Getting to the Land of Oz was hard enough. The terrain was tough and unyielding and once I managed to traverse it, I would have to climb the Wall of Itherium, a 300-foot high border meant to fend off magical beasts and gods alike, and one of Hypnos's best defenses to protect his throne in the Emerald City from harm.

There were ways through the Wall, though. I knew of one, and my friend Gyda, who lived high atop the trees in the Mountain Realm, used to speak of another that sounded like it was easier to traverse. I just hoped when I got to her house she was still there, and that I could finish my task before Epiales's grasp on Urgu was complete.

I dropped my grip on the necklace and stood, craning my neck to view the mountain above me. I could not fail. The Dream Realm would not fall while my soul stood intact. I pushed up from the ground and rushed through the gap the lava golem had made. Screams erupted from higher on the mountain as I disappeared into the trees. The monsters were still coming, and nothing could stop them, except for Nox.

CHAPTER 2
NIMUE

I was sick of the Nightmare Realm. Every moment I spent on the odd, ethereal plane ruled by the mad god Epiales was one too many. And now, there were not even the sounds of the creatures that went bump in the darkness to distract my wandering mind. The demon Etsop told me they had all been conscripted to fight in the Dream Realm. Their moans had always been unsettling, but the silence was worse.

There was an odd stillness to the Nightmare Realm, too. There used to be not only sounds, but also the wind that brushed across my face and through the abundant neon flowers. The wind now was as still as the Nightmare Realm was silent.

I wanted to get out. I needed to get out. The only reason I lingered here was because of the plan Etsop devised to send me to Earth. He got the idea from Rose, the Dreamer who apparently made it back to Earth and woke up from her unconscious stupor. Most Dreamers were not so lucky as to wake up and remained in their dreams until their bodies faded away. Etsop claimed I could possess one of them, as he had once possessed a human, and locked me inside its body.

However, that required him to be on Earth to procure a body, and my soul could not transfer there without vaporizing. So, I was left waiting in the open meadow where I once stood with Esther, the Gorgon monster—at once my mortal enemy and the only real friend I had made in a thousand years—as we searched for Epiales. I killed her when she learned that I was not her daughter's friend, but her sworn nemesis.

I didn't want to kill her. In truth, I hadn't ever wanted to kill anyone, but my hands had seen much violence. While I had no bloodlust in my veins, I had a certain... survival instinct. Survival means power, and power means fear, and fear means the death of my enemies.

In a flash and a crash, Etsop's shop appeared before me. Made from mortar and brick, it glowed a haunting green around the edges, and yet, while it glowed, it did not stick out against the vibrant neon of the rest of the Nightmare Realm.

The back door cracked open, and a tall, gangly man with deeply sunken eyes stared out at me. His smile was unnatural, as if two hooks pushed up the creases on the outside of it against the will of a perpetual frown.

"Thank you for waiting," Etsop said in a scratchy voice. "It took longer than I expected."

"I'll say," I said in a snit. "It's been several days, not a couple of hours."

"Hours, days, months, years...it's all the same to me. What matters is I have procured a vessel for you. If you'll come with me, we can get started."

I followed him through the door into his haunted pet shop. Every cage rattled on my way to the back counter, each one filled with the wild, twisted beasts of nightmares. Unlike the silence of the Nightmare Realm, the beasts inside the shop cackled, howled, and rattled their cages as I passed. Perhaps once I would have feared them, but after days of muted silence, their squawks were a welcome respite from the onslaught of my own thoughts.

"Please, lay inside the outline," Etsop said, gesturing down at the floor. "Be very precise. Otherwise, it won't work." He had moved aside a shelving unit in the middle of the store, and where there used to be feed and pet toys, there was an empty space on the floor with the outline of a human being on it, drawn in red.

"Is that blood?"

"Yes, yes, dear. I'm a demon, you realize. Most of our magic is made with blood."

"I hear blood magic is the most powerful in the world," I replied, thinking back to Esther, who had shared that tidbit with me. My old Gorgon friend racing across my mind caused a twinge in my stomach.

"That it is, my dear," Etsop said with a gentle nod and gestured again at the floor. "Now, please."

I stepped into the outline and moved to the ground, sliding onto my back. I extended my arms and shifted my feet until I was perfectly inside Etsop's outline. I was a queen once, before I became an outcast lying on the floor in a pool of blood. If it sent me back to Earth, I would put up with any degradation. All I had wanted since entering the Dream Realm was a chance to go back to Earth, to feel the true grass under my feet, and to taste the sweet taste of real food; to be rid of the artificiality that made up both the dream and Nightmare Realms, where everything was a poor imitation of the real thing.

"Where is the girl?" I asked.

"Well, I couldn't bring her with me, dearie. Bodies are fragile. She would never withstand what I was trying to do to her in this realm. She will barely survive it on Earth."

"Chelle made it through with a body," I mumbled. Chelle was the half-Gorgon daughter of Esther, and she began the downfall of my reign when she entered the Dream Realm to find her girlfriend Rose, the Dreamer.

"Well, yes, but she wasn't using blood magic nor layering it with soul magic, both of which have a habit of going pear-shaped in this place." Etsop waited for a moment before continuing. "Besides, this realm becomes less stable by the day. I only hope it survives the war."

Esther had made blood magic once. She had used the blood of a bullfrog to find Epiales's cave, but it was very simple magic, not the kind of magic we were trying to execute. Instead of arguing, I decided to just smile at him.

"What kind of girl is she?" I asked.

Etsop shrugged. "You all look the same to me. She looks like you, I suppose. Or maybe not, but enough that you will be happy, I think. I'm not sure. Please don't fill my head with trivialities. I have much more important things to do."

As long as I didn't look like Etsop, I would be happy. Of course, I would never say that out loud, but part of me thought he might be able to read my mind, because a sneer ran over his face.

"Don't move," he said. "The slightest twitch could destroy the process."

"Where is the girl?"

"She's nowhere and everywhere at once. I created a pocket dimension on Earth which will pop the minute you inhabit her brain and I return to the Earth realm to retrieve you."

"Sounds lovely."

"It won't be, but she's in a coma so it makes no difference to her," Etsop said. "Now that you are here and you've agreed to this, there are some things I need to tell you. First, you will be in my debt until such time as I release you. Agreed?"

"What does 'in your debt' mean?"

"It means you will owe me considerably. Usually I ask for a single favor, but this is a very big ask, so I will require your help in matters...until such time as I no longer need you."

"What if I die?"

"That matters little," he said. "You can be very helpful in death. I dare say you would be more helpful in death than in life."

I didn't have any other choice. Not if I wanted to return to Earth, and I desperately did. "Fine. I agree."

"Very good. Very, very good. Now, the second thing is that this poor girl's consciousness will not want to let you overtake it. It will fight to remove you like a virus. You must show it you belong, and that you are the boss of it. Show no mercy."

"How do I do that?" I asked, watching him pace above me.

"You seem to be very good at wielding power, from what little I know of you. Use that to your advantage, but do it more gently than I do," Etsop said, pointing to himself. "Reason with the body. Make it understand who you are and what you want with it. It is waiting for its master, and you must prove that you are better than its master. Do you understand?"

"I understand."

"I cannot help you. I can only show you the path. You must walk it."

I nodded. "I get it. I understand. Can we get on with this already?"

"Very well," Estop said with a tilt of his head. "Close your eyes. Remember, lay perfectly still."

I closed my eyes tightly. The next time I opened them, I would be on Earth. A smile tried to creep across my face, but I fought against it, heeding Etsop's warning to be still. He was mumbling over me, and through my eyelids I saw a looming brightness. I held myself completely still, and the brightness fell onto me. Its heat consumed me, and I fought against it, crying out in pain. *Had Etsop betrayed me? Or was this part of the process?*

As quickly as it came upon me, it was over. There was a cool breeze and I felt the floor fall out from under me. Instinctively, I opened my eyes and saw that I was falling in the darkness, suspended by the nothingness, gone from Etsop's shop and everything I once knew. Now, I was truly on my own.

CHAPTER 3

ROSE

"Let's go save my world."

Those were the last words Hypnos said to me and Jamil before he stood, took a step forward, and collapsed in a drunken stupor. Hypnos was nothing like the regal, majestic god from my memory, the shimmering god who met me in the clouds above the Emerald City and gave me his blessing—nothing like this lush at my feet.

I was used to disappointment at this point, though. Why should a god be any different? Jamil and I each grabbed one of his arms and threw it over our shoulders, hoisting him up. I placed the pink dream orb in my pocket.

When we originally entered the casino, Gwen and I both thought it was a dump, full of cobwebs and mold. Jamil, a dryad, was able to see through the illusion meant to fool humans and recognized that the casino was filled with opulence and mythological creatures.

I had been sent there to deliver a package as part of a quest given to me by the demon Etsop. Once we arrived, Gwen, a former "quest girl" we'd met along the way, opened the package to reveal a dream orb, the currency of the Dream Realm where I was once both prisoner and queen. The dream orb allowed me to see the casino as Jamil had, which was how I found Hypnos in the first place, though I had no idea why Etsop would want me to.

"Stay with him," I said to Jamil when we finally got Hypnos into his suite. He was sloppy drunk, by human or divine standards, and Jamil caught him as he mumbled and slid off the bed.

"Screw this, man," Jamil said. "I'll help you get him sober, but then I'm out. I don't need this noise."

"You can't be out!" I replied, spinning around to her. "We need you. The Dream Realm needs you."

"Girl, I don't care about the Dream Realm, and I didn't sign up for any of this. You remember what Gwen said about quest girls? I ain't about that life."

Gwen had been a quest girl in her past. She said that gods and creatures choose broken, wounded people for quests because they could be easily manipulated and had little to live for besides a little excitement. Gwen said it fit her to a tee, especially now since her best friend was dead and her boyfriend was in a mental asylum.

"Fine," I said. I didn't want a fight. "Just don't leave before I get back."

"Don't worry." Jamil's voice dripped with bitterness. "I won't leave the drunk."

"I'm not drunk!" Hypnos said, snapping out of his sleep for a moment before collapsing back on the bed.

This was stupid. Still, if I wanted to find Chelle again, I needed to get back to the Dream Realm, and Hypnos was my best shot. Everybody said that I was an idiot for wanting to go back. Everybody I met in Urgu would give their life to return to Earth, but Earth meant nothing to me without Chelle, and she was stuck in the Dream Realm.

Even with Chelle I barely cared about the world, but without her, it was meaningless.

I walked out of the suite and back down to the casino, taking the orb from my pocket and squeezing it in my hands. It gave freely, like a stress ball, and I could manipulate it in my hands, but it never broke.

I walked down the steps into the casino and spun to avoid an orcish barmaid with a plate of drinks in her hand. I had left Gwen on a bench in the lobby. With any luck, she would still be waiting for me.

I placed the dream orb on the ground and the casino immediately dropped away from me, all its glamour vanishing into gray blandness. In place of the chiming slot machines and glittering chandeliers there was nothing but overturned chairs and rotting wood.

Gwen, who was sitting on the same bench where I left her, kicked her legs under her and combed her pink-streaked black hair with her fingers. When I materialized in front of her, she skittered up to the wall, fully freaked out.

"Holy crap!" she shouted. "Where did you come from?"

"I was here the whole time," I said, quietly, trying to calm her nerves. "We all were. There's an illusion around this whole place that makes it look like a dump." I grabbed her hand and moved it to the orb with mine. "Here. See for yourself."

The darkness melted and we were again surrounded by the beauty of the casino. Gwen frowned until her bright green eyes were slits between her eyelids. "Of course. Stupid magic."

She dropped the orb and we were again in the dark, dank, drabness of the decrepit casino. I smiled at her. "I mean, it was a little cool."

"That's the problem with magic. It's all a little cool and a little stupid."

"So, does that mean you won't help us with Hypnos?" I searched her face.

She sighed. "No. It doesn't mean that, because I'm an idiot, but I'm not doing it for free. I want something out of the deal."

"I have nothing to give you," I replied.

"Not from you," she said, indignant. "From Hypnos."

"Hypnos is a bit indisposed at the moment. I don't know if he can grant favors, and I certainly can't."

Gwen folded her arms. "Then I'm not helping."

I grumbled to myself. "Fine. I hope this works." I grabbed Gwen's hand and the orb. The stale, moldy casino disappeared and in its place was the busy, beautiful one. I turned back to see Gwen staring all around her. "I guess it worked."

"I guess so, unfortunately." Gwen grimaced. "I was hoping I wouldn't be able to help and could go home, but I guess I'm in it for the time being."

I dragged her upstairs to Hypnos's suite. When we entered, I heard laughing coming from the bedroom. Two sets of laughter, guffawing at something uproariously funny. When I walked into Hypnos's room, I saw him sitting on the bed drinking a glass of water. Jamil was wiping her eyes, still laughing.

"You're back!" Hypnos said.

"You're...sober," I replied.

Hypnos shook his head. "I was never drunk, my dear, or at least, not like you think. I just had about fifty billion dreams crash into me at once. That's enough to make anybody dizzy in the head. I'm sorry for worrying you."

"I wasn't worried," I replied, but nobody was buying it. "Okay, so maybe I was a little concerned. Sue me."

"No plans to. There's work to be done." Hypnos cocked his head at Gwen. "And who is this lovely creature?"

"That's Gwen," I said. "She's an ex-quest girl, and she's willing to help in any way we need her, for a price."

"Well, not 'in any way,' but in many ways," Gwen corrected me. Her voice was terse.

"Do we need her help?" Hypnos asked, giving her an appraising look.

"I think so," I replied. "She's already been very helpful for free. I can't imagine how helpful she would be if we paid her."

Hypnos cocked an eyebrow. "I'm intrigued. All right, wow me. What can a mortal do to help me?"

Jamil chuckled. "Exactly. You're a god."

"A god who's only been on Earth a year, and now needs to go home," Gwen said. "Do you know how to get home?"

"Of course, I just have to find one of the doors my mother left for me, and everything will be fine. No problem. Barely an inconvenience. I'll be back in the Dream Realm by noon." He stopped for a moment and scratched his chin. "Of course, there is the case of my brother in the Nightmare Realm. I left him chained, but if my visions are true, he has escaped and is waging war. There will be a great disturbance in the balance of power. Epiales has grown strong—perhaps too powerful for me to take on myself."

"I know somebody who can go between the Nightmare Realm and Earth. Perhaps he can help gain you support in the Nightmare Realm," I said. "Do you know the demon Etsop?"

Hypnos spat on the ground. "A ruddy demon if I ever knew one."

"He's the worst," Gwen said. "But he could be helpful. I'll track him down and try to bring him to our side...for a price."

"Name it," Hypnos said.

"I want my boyfriend's brain mended. He...touched Chaos. Now all of his memories and thoughts are jumbled together."

"Chaos is my grandfather, one of the primordial ones. What business did you have with him?"

"I used to be a quest girl. I came in contact with all types of crazy things." Gwen rolled her eyes and put her hand on her hip. "That's my price. My boyfriend's sanity for my help."

"If you help me—and I expect your help to be substantial—then I will help you fix your boyfriend's broken brain. I just hope what you find will be worth the cost. If he has been warped by Chaos—"

"He hasn't," Gwen said. "Brad would never succumb. I know he's in there."

"Very well. If you help me, then I can make it happen for you." Hypnos reached into his pocket and pulled out two golden strands of silk, which fluttered in the recirculated air. He wrapped one in a piece of string and placed it around Gwen's neck. Then, he placed another around mine. "This is a single hair from Apate, goddess of illusion and trickery. It will allow you to see what we see, as we see it."

"Thank you," I said.

"Why do you have that?" Jamil asked. "I mean, what a weird thing to have."

Hypnos shrugged. "Gods are weird."

He picked the dream orb from my hand and placed it in Gwen's. "Show this to Etsop. It is an acknowledgement of my return, and that you speak for me. Do not offer a favor from me under any circumstances. I will not be in the debt of a trickster."

Gwen nodded. "Got it. After that, I'll be gone." She turned to Jamil. "Do you need a lift?"

Jamil shook her head. "No, I think I'm going to stay a while. You kids have fun, though."

"Very well," Hypnos said, holding his hand out for me. "Shall we?"

"You want me to come with you?" I said. "I thought I would go with Gwen—"

"She is on her own path," Hypnos replied. "Is it not your wish to enter the Dream Realm?"

I nodded. "More than anything."

"Then let us away."

I placed my hand in his giant paw. He snapped his fingers and we vanished.

CHAPTER 4
AINE

I was a prisoner. Again.

I was once a queen. I suppose I was still a queen, but one without a castle, and without freedom. No, I was not bound in a cell. I was under the ever-watchful eye of Epiales, the god of nightmares, and usurper to the rule of the Dream Realm.

Hypnos had abandoned us 100 years ago, and now we were in the hands of his deceitful brother, who devalued human and fairy kind alike. He thought us stupid and boorish, and I could do nothing when he spoke of his hatred for my people, lest he destroy me with a thought.

Because I was a queen, once and forever.

A queen knew how to be cordial and regal even in the face of a despot. I have known my share of usurpers and despots. They lusted for power as they bellowed and bragged, hoping their boisterous attitude would make up for their illegitimate claim to the throne. I feared despots because they tended to lash out like wounded dogs when questioned. One question would lead to others, and the house of cards that held up their rule would crumble under them.

Epiales took up occupancy in the trickster god Loki's temple, situated in the center of a misty, stench-ridden bog. Swampy vines twisted and tangled on the walls. He drummed his fingers on the corroded black throne rotting beneath him.

"It will be glorious," he mumbled to me as I fluttered in the air so I could maintain eye contact with him. Like a mangy dog, you could not break eye contact with a despot, or they will assume dominance and see you as weak. Weakness was death with a usurper. Despots needed strong allies to solidify their claim to the throne. Then again, you could not be too strong, or you would be a threat to their rule, and they would destroy you on the spot.

"What would be glorious, my lord?" Courtesy was the easiest way to comfort a despot. A smile and a gentle tilt of the head went a long way to ease their troubled minds.

He had been silent for a long while, but he often liked to wrinkle his brow and stare off into space, then come back with a proclamation as if he was still trying to convince me he would be a strong ruler. As a strong ruler with no doubt of my claim to the throne of the fairy realm, he seemed to need my approval of him more than he should, given his position as a god.

"My rule," he said, determined. "This place, Urgu, has never lived up to its potential under the rule of my brother."

His lip curled into a snarl as he said the word "brother." I did not know anything about his relationship to Hypnos, but Epiales's tone when speaking about him indicated hatred. And yet something else behind his eyes betrayed a deep-seated fear at a potential confrontation with Hypnos.

After listening to him for hours, I had gathered that he

worried Hypnos was more powerful than he was. Despots could never reveal their fears. They had to appear flawless and perfect at all times, or they faced a takeover from the conniving among them.

"Do you not believe me?" Epiales said, leaning toward me.

"Yes, your majesty." I replied with the lightest voice I could muster. "I believe every word. Urgu has been without a god to rule over it for too long."

"And the only logical choice is me to rule it, as my brother is indisposed. Isn't that correct?"

I nodded. "Of course, your majesty. Only you have the power to rule Urgu properly."

"Hrm," Epiales said. "You always say the right things, fairy. I can see why you have maintained power for so long."

I smiled appreciatively. "I hope to help you rule for an eternity as well."

"Do you?" His eyes narrowed.

My smile broadened. "Of course, my lord."

"Good, because there is something I need from you, my dear."

I swallowed. "And what is that?"

"There is a spell, one that only the fairies know— one which can kill anything at will, even a god."

The thought of it triggered a memory in my subconscious, but I couldn't access it. A shiver ran through me as my thoughts drifted to the crack of lightning from my past. "I do not know such a spell."

"I hope you are wrong," Epiales said. "For it is the reason you are still alive. It is a secret passed from fairy queen to fairy queen as far back as I can remember, and you are the only queen in Urgu. Even the gods do not know this spell."

"But you must have other spells that can kill."

"I do, but I fear they will not work in the coming confrontation, and I need all I can find to gain the upper hand."

"I will try to remember the spell for you."

He stared deeply into my eyes. "See that you do."

Footsteps behind me broke my concentration and I turned to see who disturbed us. In my time in Loki's Castle I had not seen another visitor. I gulped loudly when I saw the hulking visage of Agrona standing in the hallway. Her glowing white eyes lit up the dank darkness and electrified the air around her.

"My queen!" Epiales said, rushing toward her. He held out his arms and Agrona gathered him into hers and squeezed him tightly, lifting him into the air with a long and passionate kiss.

"What are you doing here?" Epiales said. "I thought we agreed you would stay in your keep until every last monster from my realm was through the portal."

"This is true, my love," Agrona said. "But I could not wait another moment without seeing you. It has been a century, and one more second was too much to bear."

"So sweet, my love." Epiales smiled. "Can you please put me down now?

Agrona stole another kiss from him. She was a mountain compared to Epiales, easily twice his size. When she had stolen a third kiss, the goddess dropped him, and her eyes turned to me. "What is she doing here?"

"She is my guest, my love."

Agrona's steps shook the whole temple as she moved

toward me. "She came to me with Hera and took the Book of Souls from me."

Epiales held up his hand. "And she brought it back to me. She pledged her loyalty."

"Her loyalty is fleeting and worthless." Agrona raised her fist over her head. "Let me smash her like the bug she is."

"Help!" I shouted. The sound eked out of me before I could think. I couldn't help it. The Mountain goddess had ripped Hera apart with barely a thought, and Hera was the most powerful being I had ever met. The fear coursing through my body was palpable.

Epiales smiled calmly and stepped forward. "My love, I appreciate it, but she has never pursued any ill will toward me, and we need partners if we are to take over Urgu. I would like to have subjects under my rule, which means taking the throne without having to kill everyone. After all, she rules the Land of Oz, and their partnership is essential to avoiding a bloodbath."

Agrona sneered. "I would sooner kill everything than work with a duplicitous pixie."

"I know, my love," Epiales said, running his fingers down her arms. "But it's just...impractical, you know? Just look at our war with Sekhmet and the Sand People. It's taking so long to get them to bow to us. I am so bored waiting."

"They will be beaten into submission soon," Agrona said with a grunt. "The Djinn keeps the portal open for us and more monsters come through every hour. As long as it stays strong, we will have the army to march against Oz and conquer. The last thing we need is a traitorous fairy in our midst."

"My dear, I can see this is upsetting to you." Epiales

turned to me. "Queen Aine, can you please give us a moment"?

"Of course." Epiales hadn't let me out of his sight in days, which meant that I couldn't relay any messages to Anansi and the resistance about the nightmare god's plans. The truth was, he hadn't shared much with me. But now I knew that Agrona's keep was unguarded, and if Sekhmet and Anansi could get there and close the portal to the Nightmare Realm, then we had a chance of ending this war.

It would be dangerous to teleport from the temple, but the chance was worth it, even if it meant Epiales would learn that I was a traitor to his cause and kill me.

CHAPTER 5
BOUDICA

Swing straight.

Aim true.

My sword sliced through the gut of a gelatinous blob and it oozed out onto the field of battle. I had been fighting non-stop at Sekhmet's side since we sent Red away into the Mountain Realm, my vacated home. I hoped she would be successful on her quest to find Nox, and rid us of the Nightmare Realm forever, but in the meantime, I had to fight.

It was as if the monsters would never stop coming. My arms were tired and my mind hazy from days of battle. I hadn't felt weary in many years, but the tide of endless battle had taken its toll.

"Behind you!" the lioness Sekhmet roared. She pulled a knife from her breastplate and flung it across the battlefield. I ducked, and watched it embed between the glowing red eyes of a shadow demon. The fire left them.

"Thank you," I replied, but there was no time to hear what she howled at me as I turned once again to the battlefield.

The white powder of the Sandlands splashed the heat of the sun on me, and my legs bowed, trying to stay upright. I looked back for a moment at the battle lines behind us. Not long ago, there had been hundreds of rows of soldiers ready for battle. Now, only a handful remained.

Aladdin, the guide that led us into the battle, had fallen days ago. He was not a fighter, but he had the heart of one. He died taking out one of these evil monsters. So many of Sehkmet's soldiers died, and while our battle lines shrank, theirs never did. They just kept coming, and we couldn't do anything about it. Soon, they would overtake our forces.

"Prepare a barrage!" Sekhmet shouted, and I heard the catapults arming behind us. The lioness raised her eyebrows at me, and I nodded. She was faster than anything I had ever seen before. She rushed forward to scoop me up, and then ran us back behind the lines as soldiers lit the rocks in the catapult and flung them into the air.

A line of archers shot arrows into the air, and for a moment there was a shadow against the brutal sun as the cascade of arrows blotted it out. The archers were the only true defense we had, but we needed to use them sparingly, for they were running out of arrows. The more of our men died, the more we had to rely on the archers to thin the attacking hordes.

"Ready the next line!" Sekhmet shouted. The soldiers shifted nervously. The fear in their hearts permeated the air around us.

"We need a break," I said to Sekhmet as she walked toward the front again.

"There can be no break. The enemy takes no breaks."

"This isn't working," I replied. "I do not like to retreat, but we have to th—"

"NO!" Sekhmet screamed. "If we fail, they will have a clear path through the Sandlands, and through Urgu."

"There won't be a Sandlands left to protect if we don't fall back. We can—"

"You can abandon my people if you choose, Boudica, but I cannot leave them to be slaughtered by the Nightmare Realm."

I stopped for a moment. "That is exactly what you are doing right now."

She spun to me, fire in her eyes. "Do not speak to me like that. You might be a queen, but I am a god."

I stepped toward her, my eyes blazing. "Then act like it."

A flash of purple light exploded in the middle of the battle lines, and when it dissipated, the purple pixie Queen Aine floated between us.

"Aine!" I shouted. "How dare you come here after siding with Epiales!"

"Do you really think I betrayed you?" she replied. "That's stupid. I didn't side with him. I'm *spying*, you idiot." She looked around. "Where is Anansi?"

"He has gone to the Emerald City to protect the throne," Sekhmet said. "We are alone in this fight while he—"

"No, that wasn't the plan!" Aine shouted. "I can't—you know what, I'm just going to have to tell you and you can do with it what you will."

"Speak!" I snapped, already weary of her circuitous ramblings. "Or leave. We have monsters to deal with."

Aine glared at me. "Agrona has left her palace, and now rests with Epiales in Loki's temple."

"Where is Loki?"

"I do not know, but that's not the point. Loki is not your

concern. You have a chance to close the portal and end this invasion right now. Agrona won't be gone long."

"How?" I said.

"She confirmed the portal was opened by the Djinn. If you can gain his loyalty, you can close the portal."

Sekhmet narrowed her eyes. "And we're supposed to trust you that you speak the truth?"

Aine scoffed. "No, Anansi was supposed to trust me, but he's not here, so all I have is you. I have to go, but please, this is your only chance."

With that, Queen Aine vanished in a cloud of purple dust, leaving us alone with her message.

"What do you think?" Sekhmet asked me.

I looked out on the battlefield. There were hundreds of monsters coming toward us. They would never stop unless we closed the portal. "I think we should tell your soldiers to fall back, and then you and I go to Agrona's castle to end this."

"The line must hold." Sekhmet growled.

"Sekhmet, they can barely hold on even with us here. If we go, then they are going to be slaughtered. Let them retreat, find shelter, and when we return, we can find them again, regroup, and—"

"Okay," Sekhmet said. She turned to a tall woman with golden eyeliner smeared down her cheeks. "General Tyoli. Bring them back. Retreat and regroup somewhere you can dig in and wait for us. They *must* follow you, do you understand?"

General Tyoli nodded. "I understand."

Sekhmet turned to me. "Let us away."

I grabbed onto her. "Ready when you are."

She picked me up like I was a ragdoll and sped us away

through the line, past the Nightmare Realm monsters. I sliced through as many as I could with my blades. We had finally caught a break—maybe—and we would not miss our chance to end this accursed war.

CHAPTER 6
ROSE

After leaving the hotel in Reno, Hypnos and I reappeared in a dingy alleyway. My legs shook from the experience. I did not like teleporting. It zapped my energy and sent my stomach into my mouth.

"Are you okay?" Hypnos asked. "Traveling so far so fast can be traumatic for people."

I nodded. "I'm okay. Where are we?"

"Philadelphia. The closest door to the Dream Realm from Reno."

"Closest?" I asked. "How many doors are there?"

"Six, at last count. My mother created them eons ago to find me anywhere she might roam."

"Your mother?"

"Nox. Goddess of darkness. She endowed both me and my brother, Epiales, with our inheritance. Control of nightmares for him, dreams for me. This gate is guarded by Mydnyte, the most vicious and loyal of all my mother's minions. However, also the most reasonable."

We walked past a green dumpster and through the alleyway. The chipped bricks and weathered shutters could use a fresh coat of paint, but it was not without its charm. "What are we looking for?"

"A door. There it—"

He didn't finish his sentence before his face dropped and he rushed over to what might have been a door, once. All that remained was some wooden beams snapped and destroyed, piled in a heap at the end of the alleyway.

Hypnos dropped to his knees. "What—what happened here?"

"I'm so sorry," I said, placing my hand on his shoulder.

"It was your father," a voice hissed from behind us. I turned to see a black cat leap from the ledge of the building onto the ground. "He destroyed every entrance into the Dream Realm after—after the incident."

It didn't take me long to realize that the cat was talking, nor did it confuse or startle me, not after all I had seen. Hypnos frowned. "What incident?"

Mydnyte paced across the alley like a predator stalking wounded prey. "Some time ago I let one through the door to Urgu, endangering all of the Dream Realm, and when your father found out...he was not pleased."

"These doors are meant for emergencies," Hypnos said, picking himself off the ground. "And this is an emergency. I suppose I will have to find another entrance."

"Good luck," the cat said, licking its paw. "They have all been destroyed."

Hypnos shook his head. "No, that's impossible. The only one who could do this is—he wouldn't..."

"He did."

"I don't believe you."

"Check for yourself," the cat said.

"I will." Hypnos turned to me. "I will be right back."

With the snap of his fingers, Hypnos vanished into the

ether, leaving me alone in the alley with the loquacious black cat. "How am I supposed to get home now!" I shouted, throwing my hands in the air.

"That's gods for you," the cat said, licking the paw that was nearly bald from her attention to it. "They bring you along until you are not useful to them anymore and then they abandon you. Do you know how long I've guarded that door?"

"No."

"Me either," I noticed the cat was listing to one side, unable to put weight on one paw. "But it was a long time. Since before this country even existed, and the door was naught but a hole in a tree stump."

"What happened to your paw?" I asked.

Mydnyte licked her wounded paw. "Erebus is not a kind god. Nox, my mistress, wasn't kind either, but she wasn't violent. She was petty and cruel like all the gods, especially those who had been around since the beginning of everything. They don't care about us, or anything. We are mere playthings to them."

"Is that who hurt you? Erebus?"

The cat looked away. "I deserved it. I made a mistake."

I knelt down. "No, you didn't. The woman you let through? That was my girlfriend. She saved me. She brought me back."

Mydnyte looked at me from the corner of her eye. "And where is she now?"

I shrugged. "I...don't know...lost in the Dream Realm. That's why I have to get back, to save her now."

"And then who will save you?" Mydnyte asked pointedly, facing me again.

"We will save each other."

"Pitiful, and naïve. How very human." Mydnyte said with a disappointed tone in her voice.

In a flash of light Hypnos returned. "They're all gone. Every single one of them smashed to pieces."

"I told you," the cat said.

He fell to his knees "How—Why?"

"You can find out for yourself." The cat hobbled forward. "Your father gave me a message for you."

"What is it?"

Mydnyte spit up a hairball and cleared her voice. "There is only one way back. If you're ready, you know where to find me. I will not make it easy, but I can be exceedingly reasonable."

Hypnos stood. "But...that's not true. I have no idea where to find him. He's been gone since the gods left this planet. He could be anywhere in the universe."

"I doubt he went far," Mydnyte said. "There is little he looks forward to more than teaching you a lesson."

"Then why did he never reach out until now?" Hypnos asked.

"I don't know. You'll have to ask him."

"How?" Hypnos said, his hands balling into fists at his sides. "You're speaking in accursed riddles like a stupid sphinx."

"I'm sure you'll figure it out. You're a clever boy. Now, if you'll excuse me, after eons, my job is done. I get to rest now."

Mydnyte hopped onto the dumpster, and then onto a ledge, and walked away, leaving us in silence for a long moment.

"What do we do now?" Hypnos said.

I scratched my head. I had an answer, but I didn't want to say it out loud. "There is only one being who I know that keeps tabs on everything on Earth and might have an inkling of where your father might be."

"You speak of Etsop," Hypnos said with an exasperated exhale.

"That's the one, unless you have a better idea. Maybe we can even beat Gwen there."

Hypnos shook his head. "I am an immortal being. You would think that I'd know plenty of people who could help us."

"Do you?"

He dropped his eyes. "No. I admit, I don't have many friends in this realm. Or any realm, for that matter."

"Me either." I held out my hand for him, and he took it in his. "We'll figure this out together."

"And if we don't?"

I looked into his bright, pink eyes. "I once had no hope, and you gave me back my soul. If it takes me believing enough for the both of us, that's exactly what I'll do."

I smiled. I much preferred myself with a soul than without one, and I could never thank Hypnos enough for making me whole again. I would certainly try, though, especially if it meant believing in him. He was convinced all hope was lost, but I knew that hope was all we had.

CHAPTER 7
RED

Even in the bright light of midday there was a gloomy haze that fell over the Mountain Realm. The mist had been there since the first time I traveled through Boudica's land, decades ago. The sun never set on the Sandlands and it never rose on the Mountain Realm.

For a long time, nobody knew why Agrona hated the light, just that there was little light in the Mountain Realms and for that reason, many dark creatures roamed the lands there. Now we knew, of course, that she was in concert with Epiales. You had to be made of steel to survive in Agrona's world without losing your mind. Even I had trouble keeping my sanity if I stayed in the mountains for too long. If there was one person I trusted to lead me through the Mountain Realm and into the Land of Oz, it was Gyda.

Gyda was cut from a different cloth than most in Urgu. She loved the mountains and was one of the few to build a permanent home in Agrona's dark kingdom. Even Boudica was not foolhardy enough to build a structure without a solid wall around it, or with the ability to move at a moment's notice.

Gyda, however, didn't much like people, and she didn't have any fear, so her cabin in the trees suited her fine. She was agile, able to avoid the creatures that went bump in the dark. From her perch above the tree line, she could see the Wall of Itherium. I hoped she could show me a way through the impenetrable barrier so I could continue my quest.

"Gyda!" I whispered loudly as I walked toward the gnarled tree where she kept her home. "Gyda!"

There was no answer, and the rope ladder leading up to her home wasn't lowered. Nothing too unusual in that, though. These were cautious times, and Gyda was cautious on a good day. It was what kept her alive.

In a pinch, the knots on Gyda's tree could serve as climbing aids, but it was a treacherous ascent. Luckily, I had watched Gyda do it a dozen times. I placed my foot on one branch and hopped to the next, repeating this exercise until I could reach out and touch the tree house if I stretched far enough.

It was still deceptively far away. I ran my hand along the bark until I found a cavity where my fingers fit. I yanked myself over to it and found a foothold closer to the tree house. Finally, I pulled myself up to the window and rolled inside, pulling my knives out of my belt as I pushed myself to stand.

"Gyda?" There was nothing in the treehouse, but I was still on edge, as you had to be in the Mountain Realm, for a trap.

I spun around and squeezed my daggers tightly. There was no dust to indicate Gyda had been killed or kidnapped. There was no sign of struggle. The house was empty. I quieted my mind and my steps and listened in the emptiness. For a moment I heard nothing, then there was a squeak behind me, and a gust of wind rustled on my left side.

I was not alone.

Whoever was in the treehouse with me was in hiding, waiting to pounce. Invisibility can be a great gift, but it can also be a crutch. It can make you sloppy and heavy on your feet. You didn't have to do anything to be sneaky when you couldn't be seen, and that was your downfall.

The floor creaked once again, and I struck at the spot with a high kick. I didn't know what I hit, but whatever my foot connected with let out a howl. It was thick and fat. Before it could recover, I smashed against it with a round-house, and then kneed it in what felt like the gut. A thick burst of air escaped it and there was a loud crash on the ground.

"Show yourself!" I screamed, but there was only silence. I kicked at the invisible beast but there was no response. "Crap."

I reached down and felt the heavy beast sleeping soundly. I would have to tie it up before it woke up if I wanted to know where Gyda went, and whether the monster had a part to play in her disappearance.

As I passed the window to find the rope ladder to tie up the beast, I caught sight of the Wall of Itherium. Beyond it, in the far distance, was the Emerald City, my home for so long, and where I would find the end of my tale, if I could ever make it there.

CHAPTER 8
NIMUE

I floated in the ether for a long while, lost in the darkness around me, but eventually, a pinprick of light flickered in the distance. I swam toward it. Coming closer, I noticed it was not simply light, but a small park filled with flowers and trees, drifting aimlessly.

I placed my foot on the ground. Suddenly the ground spread out around me, and the darkness disappeared. There were small children playing, and lovers sitting down eating a picnic lunch. An old man flew something into the air that I did not recognize, and a young woman flung a disc as her dog ran to catch it.

"Who are you?" a young voice asked.

I turned to see a girl of no more than ten, with bright red hair. Her eyes shimmered like emeralds and her skin was as pale as ivory, save for the freckles speckling her cheeks and arms. Nobody else took notice of her, or me, so I knew her interest in me meant something. I knelt to her eye level.

"My name is Nimue. What is yours?"

"Bernadette." She placed her hands on her hips and puffed out her chest. "Bernadette Howard."

I smiled. "It's very nice to meet you. I haven't come across a child in a long time."

In the Dream Realm, even the youngest-looking children could be a hundred or a thousand, but since there had not been a single new inhabitant there for a hundred years, even those who were new to Urgu were ten times older than Bernadette in spirit.

"I can't say the same to you, ma'am, being nice to meet you, that is. I know everybody who's supposed to be here, and you're not one of them."

Etsop told me to be mean, controlling, and dominant, but I couldn't bear the thought of being cruel to such a young girl. I decided that against my baser instincts I would attempt compassion. I was the intruder in this place, after all. Besides, Etsop was not the paragon for how to possess a body, given the grotesque, warped creature he became in the end.

I nodded slowly. "That's true. I have come from a far-off land, my dear, to befriend you, and help you walk again."

Bernadette shook her legs. "I don't know what you're talking about, lady. I can walk just fine, thank you very much."

I patted the grass on the ground. "In here, yes, but out there, in the real world, you have been sleeping for a long time, and I would like to help you move again. Wouldn't that be nice?"

Bernadette squinted at me. "I don't know. We're not supposed to let anybody in 'cept Bernadettes, and you're not a Bernadette. You told me so yourself."

I smiled. "And who said you couldn't let anyone in but Bernadette?"

"SHE did, obviously!"

"Can you lead me to her?"

"Course I can. I'm ten, not two. Follow me."

Bernadette kicked her leg into the air and spun around. She stomped away and I followed her. At the edge of the park was a small gate. Bernadette unlatched it and walked through. When I passed through after her, a gust of air washed over me. I nearly fell over. A massive tornado blotted out the sun, and I was certain we were done for.

"Come on!" Bernadette screamed, running toward an old barn in the distance.

I ran behind Bernadette until we reached the barn. The shutters slammed against the windows, crashing upon them over and over again. The wooden siding of the barn creaked and twisted until a huge section snapped off and flew through the air.

"Help me!" she screamed.

Bernadette was trying to lift a door embedded in the ground. I wrapped my hands around the handle and together we yanked it open and rushed inside. The door slammed closed behind us.

"Grab the other end!" she shouted through terse breaths.

Bernadette pulled up one side of a long wooden beam and I picked up the other and we shoved it into a latch that held the door in place. Once it was secure—though the wind beat upon it mercilessly—Bernadette lit a small lantern and descended into the basement.

"Don't touch anything," she growled. "Don't talk to anyone."

"Okay."

At the bottom of the stairs, the lantern illuminated a small room with a dirt floor. I heard whimpering in the corner, where a younger version of Bernadette huddled next to an older woman wearing a floral print dress.

"It's okay, my love." The woman rocked the young girl gently. "It will all be okay."

Younger Bernadette cried out and whimpered loudly as barn crunched and snapped and the wind howled overhead.

"We lost everything," ten-year-old Bernadette said with a sigh. "That's why we moved to California. Stupid idea. If only—" She stopped talking and simply sighed loudly. "Come on. It's over now."

I paused to listen and realized she was correct. The sound of the snapping and tearing from the tornado was over. "That was quick."

"Time moves differently here." Bernadette walked up the stairs and placed the lantern back on its hook. She grabbed onto the beam and looked at me. "Come on."

I grabbed on to the other side of the beam and we lifted it. The door opened with ease and we stepped outside, no longer on the farm but on a beach. The warm breeze blew the salty smell of the ocean into my nose.

"That's Kyle. He's our boyfriend." Bernadette pointed to a blanket, where a young man with a concave chest and thick glasses sat reading a book. "He's not much to look at, but he's nice to us."

A young woman with long, dark red hair came running from the shore and grabbed a towel. She was sopping wet from the ocean, and after toweling off her face, put on a pair of thick, black glasses. Her freckles were more prominent than little Bernadette's.

"Don't you ever get tired of the water?" Kyle said. "It's not even warm."

"Feels great to me," Bernadette said, dabbing at herself with the towel. "What time is it?"

Kyle picked up a strange, thin, black, brick-like object and stared at it for a moment. "Just about four. We should go."

Older Bernadette rolled her eyes. "Just a little while longer."

Kyle shook his head. "I have work. I shouldn't have even come here today. The ocean is so far from home. We'll have to rush." He kissed Bernadette gently. "But I just can't say no to you."

Young Bernadette turned to me. "It wasn't his fault."

"What wasn't?"

"Any of it. It was my idea. Come on," Bernadette said as we followed older Bernadette and Kyle to a horseless carriage and watched as they placed their gear in the trunk. The parking lot was filled with horseless carriages, but there wasn't a horse in sight. Bernadette didn't seem concerned and opened the back door of the carriage and slid inside. "Let's go."

"What is this?" I asked.

"It's a car, dummy." Bernadette closed the door. "Ain't you ever seen a car before?"

"I—have not," I admitted.

Kyle and Bernadette lowered themselves into the front seat, with Kyle on the left and Bernadette on the right, but young Bernadette took little mind of them. "Where have you been livin'?"

"In a dream, I suppose you could say."

"Me too. A nightmare, more like it."

The car jerked to life with a roar and pulled forward like it was powered by magic. As it did, the day turned to night, and Kyle continued down a dark road. I had never seen anything like it. There had been talk through the Dream Realm of somebody building a car, but it was nothing like this.

"It wasn't his fault," Bernadette said. "He just wanted to give us a nice day."

"What wasn't his fa—"

A white light came upon us, and with a sudden jerk we were slammed into the air, rolling upon ourselves as the car crashed and flipped, then tilted on its side. Bernadette was bloodied and barely breathing, but Kyle...his eyes were open, motionless, and dead.

"Come on." Bernadette opened the door and pulled herself up through the door. I followed her but when I came to, I wasn't on the side of the road. I was in a white room filled with windows that played hundreds of different images.

"I don't want to die," young Bernadette said.

I caught up to her. "I don't want you to die."

Bernadette turned to me. "She's not coming back, is she?"

I sighed. "No. I don't think so."

Bernadette looked carefully at me. Her green eyes shone brightly. "And if you take over, then we won't die?"

I shook my head. "No, you won't."

She furrowed her brow at me. "And you won't forget us?"

I shook my head even harder. "Never."

She pointed to a black chair in the middle of the room. "Then sit."

"Thank you." The moment my back came in contact with the chair, a light flooded through me and I woke up. Every part of me ached and burned. My lungs felt like I was on fire, they burned so badly, and I coughed violently to void the air from them. I recognized the stands from Etsop's store. I looked down at my pale arms, speckled with freckles.

"Welcome back," Etsop said as he stood over me.

"Ow," was all I could say as I slowly worked myself to standing. I ached everywhere and my bones cracked, but it was glorious. I could feel it. I was on Earth. It had worked.

As I attempted to steady my wobbly legs, the bell over the door rang. A woman with pink hair like those of the Mountain People walked inside with purpose.

"Excuse me," she said. "I'm looking for Etsop."

Etsop stepped forward. "I am he. How may I help you?"

"My name is Gwen. I'm friends with Rose and Hypnos. We need your help."

The blood rushed to my head, and I lost the grip on the counter. I fell back into the inky blackness.

CHAPTER 9
AINE

I flashed away from the desert battlefield of the Sandlands and back into the dark recesses of Loki's temple. It had only been a couple of minutes, and when I fluttered back to the throne room, Agrona and Epiales were still in the middle of a conversation.

Good. That meant they wouldn't have noticed me leaving. Even in the best circumstances, leaving the temple would have been tricky. Finding a place to teleport to in the middle of a war was harder than I imagined.

"Oh, good," Epiales said with a smile as I floated into the room. "You're back."

"Back?" I replied with a lump in my throat. "What do you mean?"

Agrona scoffed and sat down on the throne, staring daggers at me.

Epiales smiled at her and then looked back at me. "You don't have to play coy with me. I'm very aware that you never intended to help me, but that did not mean you could not be of use to us."

"You're wrong. I'm completely loyal to—"

"Don't anger me, pixie!" Epiales said. "You have been a great help to us, even if it was against your will, and for that I am inclined to let you live—though with great pain—but if you do not stop your lies I will destroy you right now."

"If you're going to accuse me of something," I said, holding my head high. "I should at least know what it is, plainly and clearly."

"Do you think I am dumb, that I did not know you would go running off to your compatriots at the first chance?" Epiales took a step toward me. I tried to flutter away, but I was held in place, unable to move. I tried to vanish, but I couldn't do anything. I was trapped. "I planned all of this, every moment, to give you a chance to set your friends up with our plot."

"Plot?" I asked.

"To destroy them, of course. Without Sekhmet, the conquest of this world will be easy. None will dare question my rule if there are no gods to turn to for safety."

"You said you would free us all."

Epiales let out a laugh. "Yes, I suppose I did say that. But I will tell you plainly now, I have no intention of letting you leave. In fact, I intend to take the Heart of Urgu and bring even more Dreamers to me, maximizing my power. I can use it to take control of every realm the gods hold precious. You are only good to me as a power source, and the gods are only good to me dead."

"You're crazy."

A wicked smile crested over Epiales's face. "No one can see reality as it truly is and not go a little mad. I had time in the silence to see the true nature of this universe, and it lies in power."

"You won't get away with this."

"Who's going to stop me? You?" Epiales snapped his

fingers and a glass jar formed around me. It must have had flecks of iron embedded in it because I could not escape it. Epiales reached out and grabbed the jar, bringing it to his face. "Don't worry, pixie. I will keep you alive to see every single one of your compatriots vanquished, and once there is no hope left in you, I will decide what your fate should be. It depends on whether you give your mind to me."

"Never!" I slammed against the sides of the glass jar, but it was no use. I was a prisoner, and worse, I had just led Sekhmet into a trap designed to kill her. *What have I done?*

BOUDICA

Sekhmet sped through the trees and forests of the Mountain Realm, up the side of the unscalable mountain that Agrona called home, and to her front door. When we reached the top of the mountain, she dropped me on the ledge. The foul stench of Agrona's evil invaded my nostrils.

"We are here," Sekhmet said.

A rancid mouth stared back at me from where the door to the castle was supposed to be, like a homeless clown that had drunk himself to death and left its mouth hanging open as a testament to its love for booze. I pushed on the lips and pulled the bottom one down to the ground. As I did, a bumpy tongue rolled out onto the ledge and continued off the edge of the cliff.

"This is horrid." The smell of rancid cheese wafted out of the mouth.

"Let's go," Sekhmet said, stepping onto the squishy tongue. It undulated under our feet. "It's not going to get any better."

She was right. The putrid stench worsened until my

knees wobbled. A harsh blue light fell on us from the end of the hallway, which eventually broke into a throne room. Even when elevated by several steps, the gnarled throne was dwarfed by the pulsating and swirling blue portal against the wall. The gateway rose thirty feet into the air and was crusted by a black, smoky border.

"Be careful," Sekhmet said. "Agrona would have left traps for intruders."

"Or maybe the trap was Aine telling us to come here," I posited.

Sekhmet shook her here. "Aine seemed confident that she was not being duped."

"And what if she was duping us?" I said.

"Anansi trusts her, so I trust her. Now be silent as I perform the ritual."

Sekhmet drew an oil lamp from her belt and held it into the air. Sekhmet once held a Djinn captive at the border between the Sandlands and the Mountain Realm. However, it had been stolen by Agrona, who used it to open a portal to the Nightmare Realm and unleash their monsters upon us. If I trusted anyone to control the Djinn, it was Sekhmet.

"Will that bind the Djinn to the lamp and close the portal?" I couldn't resist asking.

"That is the hope," Sekhmet said, thumbing the lamp. *"Juni almisbah, 'ana mulzim bik wa'atsil bika. Juni almisbah, 'ana mulzim bik wa'atsil bika. Juni almisbah, 'ana mulzim bik wa'atsil bika!"*

"NO!" A thunderous explosion rocked through the room. The blue-black shadow from around the portal formed a face, complete with bright yellow eyes and long black hair pulled back into a ponytail. "I will not be bound again!"

"*Juni almisbah, 'ana mulzim bik wa'atsil bika,*" Sekhmet growled. "I bind you, genie. I bind you to this holy relic for a million years."

The genie laughed. "That relic is nothing but an old oil lamp. It is not holy."

Sekhmet's lioness eyes narrowed, and a sneer crossed her face. "I am a goddess. Anything I touch is a holy relic if I desire it. Now, I bind you! *Juni almisbah, 'ana mulzim bik wa'atsil bika!*"

Nothing happened. "*Juni almisbah, 'ana mulzim bik wa'atsil bika!* Genie, I bind you!"

"Why isn't this working?" I shouted.

"Because!" the genie boomed again. "I am a servant to Agrona, and work for her freely. She bound me to her in exchange for three wishes. Until they are all gone, I cannot be bound to another."

"How many wishes has she used, Djinn?"

"Two. She has one other, which she has promised to use to free me."

"And if she doesn't?"

The yellow eyes turned to me. "Then it will be nothing but another betrayal of the gods."

"But I will!" a voice snarled behind me. Agrona stood in the entrance, an evil smirk on her face. "I knew you would come, sister. Foolish."

"Agrona!" Sekhmet said in genuine fear. I was not the only one who feared the Mountain goddess.

I rolled to the side as Sekhmet rushed Agrona. Sekhmet locked her in an arm brace as I turned to the Djinn.

"What did she wish for?" I asked him.

"I cannot say," the Djinn replied. "It would go against my moral code."

My eyebrows shot up. "So you let millions of monsters into this realm and now you have a moral code?"

"I always have. That it does not match yours is of no concern of mine."

"And yet you work for a butcher!" I screamed. "Agrona and Epiales are trying to enslave the whole of the Dream Realm. You see no problem with that?"

"No price is too great for my freedom," he growled.

"Then help me, and I will set you free right now."

The Djinn scoffed. "I have heard that before."

"I swear. I will free you on the condition that you grant me the other two wishes once you are free, and then you will be free of everything and able to go anywhere you wish, bound by nothing and no one."

Sekhmet screamed out. A snap echoed through the air and a moment later her body skidded across the ground. It stopped at my feet, its lion head twisted grotesquely. She was dead, and a moment later she turned to dust.

"It won't matter," the Djinn said. "She is too powerful for you."

"But she's not too powerful for you," I said. "Even Sekhmet feared your power."

"No. She is not. I could fight her, but I won't."

"Queen Boudica," Agrona snarled. "You were such a good little soldier of mine for so long. You helped keep this place strong. It is so disappointing that you have sided with the enemy."

I stood, ready to fight. "Sekhmet is not the enemy. She sides with freedom. You want nothing but power."

"Power is everything!" Agrona said. "There is nothing if there is not power."

An idea hit me. "So you value power more than freedom, then?"

"Are you stupid?" Agrona scoffed. "Of course I do."

I pointed to the portal. "But the Djinn is power incarnate, and you offered him freedom once you are done with him. How can you give that freedom if he is more powerful than you?"

"More powerful than me? That is laughable. Epiales and I are the most powerful beings in this realm. None can stand against us, and with the power of the Djinn, we will rule forever."

"Forever?" the Djinn said. "You truly never were going to offer my freedom, were you?"

Agrona scoffed. "I still have one wish left, Djinn, and you cannot break our pact until I use it. If you are very good, I will let you free...before the end of time."

The Djinn turned to me, then eyed the oil lamp in Sekhmet's hand. He nodded at me, and I lunged for it. *"Juni almisbah, 'ana mulzim bik wa'atsil bika. Genie, I bind you!"*

"What?" Agrona said. "What's happening?"

The blackness around the portal folded into the oil lamp. As it did, the walls around the castle began to crumble.

"Get me out of here!" I shouted as Agrona stomped toward me.

"Not until you fulfill your bargain. Free me!"

"Fine!" I shouted. "Djinn, I wish that you were free!"

"NOOO!" Agrona said, screaming.

But it was too late. The entire castle exploded with a white light and thunderous jolt, and Agrona was blown out of its walls just as they began to collapse. The Djinn stood before me, holding the weight of the walls and mountain with his back.

"I believe you have another wish, fearless one."

"Get me out of here and back to Sekhmet's people!" I cried.

"As you wish."

The Djinn snapped his fingers, and we were gone. In the instant before, I watched the portal to the Nightmare Realm collapse upon itself. Agrona's castle was sucked into nothingness.

CHAPTER II
RED

Gyda kept extensive maps of everywhere she traveled. I admired this about her. Living high in the trees allowed her to see much, but like few others that I knew, she also traveled across the whole world. Nearly every soul in Urgu made a pilgrimage to the Obsidian Spindle at some point in their afterlives, but few traveled beyond that. The spire could be seen from most of the Dream Realm, like a beacon in the dark. Very few who traveled to the Spindle ended up traveling back, which is what made the Land of Oz so powerful. Almost all Dreamers lived inside its borders.

For those of us stuck in Urgu, the Obsidian Spindle was the sole hope for salvation. If we made it there before our bodies died on Earth, the Fates could send us home. Few were so lucky. The rest of us were bound to this place forever.

I was one of the unlucky ones.

But the Fates took pity on me and gifted me the insight to always know the right course of action, even if I couldn't articulate it. It helped me in my service to the realm, but since I'd left the service of Oz, it was admittedly difficult to discern the truth from the nerves. I thought I was headed in the right direction, but where was it pulling me? I had no faith in myself. I used to be so certain of everything. Now I doubted and questioned it all.

I was certain Rose was the savior of Urgu, that she would bring about peace—but she was murdered mere moments into her reign. I had also been certain Ozma would return to the throne, but she was dusted before she ever came close.

Could I even trust my gut anymore? Could I trust anything?

I stared out of the treetop window at the Wall of Itherium, the magical barrier between the mountains and the Land of Oz, where I would find my destiny. Behind me, the invisible monster stirred, the body shaking the floor under it. I spun to watch the ropes twist around themselves, to no avail, until they finally came to a stop.

"Gods damn it!" a voice squealed. "Let me out of these —Are you the one who captured me?"

"Who, me?" I said.

"There is none other here I could be speaking to. So yes, red one. I mean you."

I knelt down next to the ropes. I had felt the size of the beast as I was tying it up, and I was careful to give its hairy body a wide berth. "I'm sorry, but I do not speak to imaginary creatures."

"I'm not imaginary! I'm invisible!"

I nodded. "Be that as it may, unless I can see you, I cannot answer you."

"And yet, you speak to me now," the monster grunted.

I shrugged. "If you want to continue this conversation, I suggest you reveal yourself."

The floor wobbled as the monster pounded the floor in fury. "You don't make the rules! I make the rules! Do you know who I am? How dare you—I should—I could—" I stood up and walked away as it continued to squawk. The floorboards creaked beneath with its movements. "I should —How—Are you listening to me?"

I stretched. "I can't hear you."

"Patently false!" the monster screamed. "When I get out of here, I'm going to—You just wait—" The ropes began to twist again, as the monster struggled. "Who tied these, King Gordius?"

"You will find it quite impossible to escape, imaginary creature. I am an expert at tying knots. I have never met my equal."

"You have never met me then. I'm going to—I just need to—If I just—gods damn it! I am the Cheshire—king of the cat beasts! You will not treat me like this!" The creature sighed after it had tired itself out. "Fine. If I reveal myself will you untie me?"

I shook my head. "No, but I will at least parlay with you."

A long grunt finished with an invisible paw turning into a purple one with long purple hairs stringing up the crea-ture's pudgy body, until whiskers appeared alongside a long, misshapen mouth filled with dozens of razor-sharp teeth. Yellow glowing eyes stared out at me, larger than the creature's small head should allow.

"You are hideous," I said. "What horrible thing dreamed you up?"

"Not a dream, sweetheart, a nightmare. And a very violent one, if I am honest."

"Well, then, I should make sure to keep you tied up if you are violent."

The purple cat-like creature flopped around on the

floor, tantruming until it finally came to rest again with a long screech. "Let me out of here!"

I shook my head in disappointment. "That is not polite."

The beast rolled over and leaned against the wall behind it. "What do you want of me?"

I pulled Anansi's spider out of my pocket. He told me it would reveal the truth to me when I needed it. I had tested it on myself. It glowed blue with the truth, and red with a lie. I placed it on the table in front of me. "What have you done with Gyda? Where is the woman who owns this house?"

The beast shook its head. "The house was empty when I came upon it." The spider glowed blue. *The truth.*

"And you decided to squat in it?"

"Lady, I am not dying for the Nightmare Realm, and I sure ain't dying for Epiales's invasion plan. I came to the Dream Realm like he said, but death can come to dumber monsters than ones who deserve it."

Another blue light. The truth yet again. I was surprised the monster was not filled with deceit. I crossed my arms. "I must admit, I did not expect to see such self-preservation among your kind."

"And what kind is that? Do you think all monsters the same?"

"Not exactly." I thought for a moment. "Though honestly, I admit that I am not sure what kind you are."

"Exactly," Cheshire scoffed. "Racist."

"Am not. I just...never thought about it before."

"Course you haven't. That's what they all say. Now, what do I have to do to get out of these ropes?"

"Promise you will not thrash about or lash out if I do."

"That I can promise. I won't hurt you." The spider glowed red. *A lie.*

I laughed. "You're lying, or at least you think you're lying. Truth is, though, that you couldn't hurt me if you tried." The spider glowed blue. *I was telling the truth.*

"You are very cocky. I eat cocky for breakfast."

"Not on this day. Now promise and mean it."

"Fine. I promise." The spider glowed blue. "Now, let me go."

"That is not all I wish. I wish to know your plan, and Epiales's plan for this realm."

"Honey, I'm flattered you think I'm privy to that kind of information, but all I got was a marching order and a destination. Far as I know, Epiales is angry at his mother that his brother got such a nice place to live and he was left in the dark with us nightmares." The spider glowed blue. He was telling the truth. *He was useless.*

"So he wishes destruction upon us?"

"Probably," the cat grumbled. "Or maybe just some good old-fashioned chaos. I always did love chaos."

"Seems like a long way to go for sibling rivalry."

"You must not have any family."

I didn't, but I certainly wouldn't have told him even if I did. "If you cannot be helpful, I'm afraid you have no bargaining chip." I grabbed the map and spider from the table and put them back in my pocket. "I'm sure somebody will be along to find you. Perhaps Gyda can boil you into a stew. I have seen you monsters from the Nightmare Realm die. You don't so much break into dust as turn into goop. I wonder how it tastes."

"Wait!" Cheshire said. "I can't be found by any others. If any from the Nightmare Realm find me, they'll kill me for sure. They are not kind."

I pressed one of my knives against the cat's chin. "As will I, if you waste any more of my time."

"The map," he stammered. "You took a map from the table. What were you looking for?"

I scoffed. "Like I would tell you, monster."

"Are you looking for a way through the Wall of Itherium?"

I pressed my knives further into his fur. "How did you —? What do you know of the Wall?"

"I know there's a flaw in it, and not too far away. That's how I found this place. Bunch of monsters were looking for it as a way to launch an attack on the Land of Oz without going through the Sandlands. It was small—real small, but we've been working to open it up. If you let me go, I will take you to it."

I crinkled my brow. "If you guide me into the Land of Oz, then I will decide whether to release you or not."

"I'll show it to you, then you release me for sure," the cat said. "That's a good deal, best you'll get from anyone in the Nightmare Realm."

"Very well." I pulled the spider out of my pocket and held it up to his face. "Agreed. If you lead me into a trap, though, I will kill you before they capture me. If you lead me into the Land of Oz, I will let you go."

The monster nodded. "Agreed."

The light glowed blue. He was telling the truth, or at least he believed he was.

CHAPTER 12

NIMUE

"I need your help," a woman's voice said as I blinked open my eyes.

"Yes," Etsop's voice replied. "You have said that already."

I stood on shaky legs. No matter how many times I rubbed my eyes, my sight remained slightly blurry.

"Ah, my dear Bernadette," Etsop said, loping toward me. "There you are."

"What are you—" Then I remembered that I was a new person now, in a new body, with a new name, and if any found out I was the Wicked Witch Nimue then I would be in a heap of trouble. "What happened to me?"

"You stood up too fast. The blood rushed to your head." Etsop leaned forward and whispered to me. "You haven't had blood in a long time. You must be more careful."

I nodded. "Thank you. Why are my eyes so blurry?"

Etsop wiggled a finger in the air. "Ah yes, yes. I found these when you fell." He pulled something from a nearby shelf and handed it to me. I pulled it close. It was a pair of black glasses made of thick, smooth material. I placed them over my eyes, and the minute they rested on my face I could see clearly again.

"Much better."

Etsop nodded. "I thought so."

"What is happening here?" the woman's voice said from behind Etsop. I leaned to see a pretty girl with pink hair and a perpetual snarl.

"It's okay, my dear," Etsop said. "Bernadette fell and hit her head, but everything is okay now. Right, Bernadette?"

I nodded. Pain split through my head and caused me to wince. "I'm fine. Just a little headache."

"Are you sure?" the girl said, rushing forward to help me find my balance. "He didn't hurt you, did he?"

"I resent that accusation," Etsop said with a scoff. "I couldn't hurt a fly."

"Please." She slid her hand under my arm to help me stop wobbling. She turned to him, but Etsop stared at her blankly. "I know who you are, and what you do."

Etsop chuckled. "Well that's not very difficult, darling. I have it right on the sign. I run a pet shop."

The girl let go of me and I wobbled some more. I hadn't felt the pull of Earth's gravity in many hundreds of years. Combined with the blood now coursing through my veins, it was exhilarating. "You have a pet shop with no pets?"

"We're in a down economy. Things will pick up."

"I don't have time for this," the girl said. "I came because Rose asked me to. You remember Rose. You helped her girlfriend get into the Dream Realm, and you forced her to deliver a package to Hypnos."

"Hypnos!" I shouted. I couldn't believe that the name escaped her lips. "Here?"

"See, that was weird," the girl said, glancing at me with a scowl. "But not the weirdest thing I've seen this week, so how about you cut the crap, Etsop? I need your help, but more importantly, Hypnos and Rose need your help."

I couldn't believe Rose was alive. And that she had found Hypnos. The last time I had seen the girl she was a pile of ash in an urn, and now she had found the most powerful being in Urgu—living here on Earth? It certainly made sense, but my head swirled with dizziness as I tried to process it all.

"What could your friend possibly need from a demon?" I asked the girl.

"See, at least *you* admit it. I like you." She spun toward Etsop. "I suppose I don't know what else to expect from a demon except deceit and confusion."

Etsop shrugged. "I am what I am, but you are being quite rude for someone looking for my help. What is your name again, child?"

"Gwen," she replied. "And that's all the personal information you are getting from me. As for the rudeness, I know what matters with a demon. It isn't what you say, or how you say it, it's what you're offering."

Etsop leaned toward her, his eyebrow raised. "And what are you offering?"

"This is proof I speak for him." Gwen pulled out a dream orb from her pocket. It shimmered pink. "The Nightmare Realm is invading the Dream Realm. We need you to help convince the monsters in the Nightmare Realm not to attack. In return, you will win the favor of the god of dreams."

Etsop scoffed. "You overplayed your hand. He would never offer me a favor. He knows what I would use it for."

A crack of thunder and lightning filled the room. When

the light abated, I recognized the two beings that stood in front of me immediately. Hypnos, shaggier than his reliefs, and dressed in ragged pauper clothing, was nearly unrecognizable, but next to him stood the unmistakable visage of Rose.

"Gwen!" Rose shouted, rushing to her. "You found him!"

"Of course I did," she grumbled. "What are you, checking on me?"

Rose shook her head. "No, of course not. We have pressing, urgent business with Etsop."

"So do I," Gwen said. "Or don't you remember?"

"Hypnos, so good to see you." Etsop genuflected, but it was clearly meant as a joke. "And what can I do for the God of Dreams and the Queen of Oz?"

Hypnos walked forward. "My father destroyed every door into the Dream Realm. We must find the key to unlock the Spindle. Have you an idea where my father resides?"

Etsop nodded. "Of course. I can give you the address right now...for a price."

"Careful what you ask, demon," he growled. "Nothing is worth me granting a favor to you."

"Told you." Etsop shook his head at Gwen. "Nothing like that. I just want you to take my assistant with you when you go." He pointed at me. "She may not look like much, but she will be a great asset to you."

I put my hands on my hips. "What if I don't want to go with them?" I had no interest in being around Hypnos or Rose. I had traveled across dimensions to avoid them, actually, but it was clear Etsop didn't care.

The sides of Etsop's mouth curled unnaturally. "That is not your choice, dear. You owe me...greatly. Remember our agreement?"

He was right. I did remember. "Fine," I grumbled.

"No!" Gwen said. "We don't know this person."

"I know that, Gwen," Rose said. "But we don't have much of a choice, and as far as favors go, it's a pretty small one."

"Says you," Gwen said. She narrowed her eyes at me. "But there's something about her I don't like."

"Do you have a better plan?" Hypnos asked.

Gwen said. "Well, no, but anything is better than getting a favor from a demon."

Etsop shook his head. "I would not bet on that. I have looked into the Dream Realm. It will fall soon if you are not there to help it."

"I don't believe you." Hypnos stared, resolute. "I trust my people to defend it."

"Even from your brother? He is as powerful as you in that place. You are the only being, besides your mother, who can stop him, and I doubt she will be doing anything to stop this sibling rivalry. After all, she never has before, has she?"

Hypnos grumbled. "Fine, we will take your apprentice with us."

"I didn't say apprentice," Etsop said with scorn. "She is my assistant. This isn't the Dark Ages."

"Hey!" Gwen said. "There are still apprenticeships out there."

"Fair enough," Etsop held out his bony, lanky fingers. "Do we have a deal?"

"Not a deal." Hypnos shook Etsop's hand loosely. "An accord." When Hypnos pulled back his hand, it contained a sheet of paper.

"And there you go." Etsop said. "He should be there when you get there. He doesn't go out much."

"Thank you," Rose said.

"Don't thank me. You have no idea how surly Erebus can be." Etsop sighed. "Now get out of my store, all of you. I am sick of visitors. Especially ones who smell of hope like you ruddy lot."

CHAPTER 13
BOUDICA

We reappeared atop a sand dune looking out into the vast desert.

"Where are we?" I asked the Djinn as I righted myself.

"You asked to be brought to Sekhmet's troops and thus, I have done so. It was a very poor wish, but I have granted it."

I saw a town surrounded by a makeshift wall lined with monsters. In the distance was the Sand Sea, and beyond it, the Wall of Itherium. If they beat Sekhmet's forces, they would have a clear path to the Gates of Droangor, and the Land of Oz, in less than a day.

"I must help them," I said, drawing my sword.

"Do you wish me to help you?" the Djinn asked with a grin. There was only one wish left, and I would not waste it in anything except an emergency.

I shook my head. "You are free to do what you choose."

"That's cute, but I'm still bound to you until you finish your final wish."

"Then you are free to fight."

I slid down the sand dune and rushed toward the town.

I tore through the ranks of the Nightmare Realm as I strode confidently forward. There was a time when I cowered from the likes of the nightmares, but those days were long gone. I slashed them through, happy in the knowledge that they were as black and dark inside as they were on the outside.

As I plowed through their ranks, the nightmares turned to me, their eyes shining like stars. There were too many of them. But if I were to die, I would go down fighting. Each one I took out was one less to attack the troops, and one more moment of respite for them to regain their strength.

I slashed once, twice, three times before I was overcome with the beasts. They breathed down on me, and at the moment I feared all hope was lost, a giant quake knocked the beasts away. I turned to see the Djinn blowing up the sand on either side of me.

"Go!" he shouted. "And hurry!"

The sand created a barrier against the nightmares so that I could reach the troops. I rushed through the line and leapt over the wall that protected the troops from the nightmares. The wall wobbled and shook. Those of the Sands did not build structures that lasted. They were nomads and moved like the wind across the desert.

Two guards pulled me over the wall, and I landed in the hot sand on the other side. When I pushed to my feet, one of Sekhmet's personally-trained generals, Rashida, shimmering in golden armor from her head down to her feet, met me.

"What of your mission?" she asked, straight to the point.

I stayed silent for a moment. "The gate is closed. The nightmares can no longer enter our realm."

"Praise be! And what of Sekhmet, where is she?"

I shook my head. "She didn't make it. She died in combat, gloriously, defending her people to the end."

"I see." Rashida bit her lip. "Without her, we don't stand a chance."

"Perhaps you do," a voice boomed behind me. It was the Djinn, appearing through the wall. "But that all depends on Boudica."

Rashida placed her hand on her sword. "And who are you?"

"He might be your last hope," I said. I looked around and saw barely a battalion of soldiers left out of the 10,000 we'd left. "What happened to all your soldiers?"

"We tried to regroup. We tried to fight them off, but without Sekhmet, all we could do was fall back, leaving our men to die as we rebuilt our defenses further and further back into the Sandlands."

"Well, we are here now," I said.

The earth quaked, and when the sand cleared, at the top of the hill stood Agrona, her eyes breathing white fire. "The Djinn is mine!"

Before I could blink, Agrona was down the hill and smashing through the wall. Dozens of guards flung through the air, and the Nightmare Realm monsters rushed through, taking on the ill-equipped guards.

"RETREAT!" Rashida screamed, but as soon as she'd finished giving the order, Agrona ripped her head from her body and flung it away. The rest of Rashida's body turned to dust where she had been standing. The screams of Sekhmet's soldiers rose around us, and the dust from their dead bodies fluttered through the air.

Agrona stepped forward. "Come with me, Djinn," she growled. "We have much work to do."

"I am not under your control anymore, witch. I am free."

"I still have one wish," Agrona said with a smile. "And because of that, I wish for you to watch while I destroy every one of these soldiers, and their leader watches helplessly."

"No!" I screamed. "You can't–"

"I'm sorry," the Djinn said. "She does have one wish left."

Agrona laughed. "And once I am done, I will rip you in half. We are not immortal, none of us." She snapped her head to me. "As you well know." Her eyes returned to the Djinn. "I know how to kill you. And I know how to make it quick and painless or slow and agonizing. Which would you prefer?"

The Djinn stood his ground. "You do not scare me, god. There are beings in this universe more frightening than a god."

Agrona turned her attention to me. I raised my sword, but she snapped it in half and grabbed me by the collar. "Very well. Then I suppose I will make it very painful for your new friend."

"Djinn, help!"

"I cannot. You must make a wish."

I couldn't think. I couldn't speak. Agrona gripped me by the neck and squeezed the life out of me.

"Save them," I said.

The Djinn shook his head. "I cannot interfere with Agrona's wish."

I don't want to die.

"Is that your wish?" I heard the Djinn's voice echo through my head.

Yes.

"Very well. As I live, so will you."

The earth quaked yet again, and I fell to the ground. My head hit the sand, and I felt its warmth on my neck as my mind faded into black and I lost consciousness.

What a coward I was. I could have saved everyone. I could have wished for Urgu to be free. But instead I thought only of myself. What kind of queen am I?

CHAPTER 14

ROSE

Hypnos's knees dug into my back the whole time we were driving to his father's house. It wasn't a short drive either. I glanced back at him every now and then, hoping to catch his attention, but he did little but stare out the window until we crossed over the bridge from Oakland to San Francisco.

"He would live here," Hypnos grumbled. "Pompous prick."

"What's your problem with your father?" The new girl, Bernadette, asked as she pushed up her glasses.

"You would never understand. You aren't a god."

Bernadette smiled. "No, but I've had a father. Don't much remember him, though."

"My dad is the worst," I said. "If you can't remember yours it's probably for the best."

My mom and dad were racist, homophobic twatwaffles. They were downright gleeful when Chelle disappeared. They acted like she never existed, and that I wasn't freaking gay. They tried to set me up with boys and send me to church socials so I could find the one. But I'd already found the love of my life and lost her. I was going to get her back, even if I had to deal with Hypnos digging his knees into my back until the end of time.

After several more turns through narrow, hilly streets, we finally ended up on a long, narrow lane packed to the gills on either side with cars. Gwen maneuvered through them before she stopped the car on an incline and pointed to a thin blue townhouse, squeezed from either side by two other townhomes. A dozen steps led up to its red door.

"There's no place to park," Gwen said. "I'll circle around and—"

"It's okay. Here is fine. Don't bother waiting for us." Hypnos pushed open the car door. "You and the new girl go find a diner and we'll find you when we're done."

"Are you kidding me?" Gwen said. "I'm not a chauffeur!"

"And Etsop was very clear that I was supposed to come with you," Bernadette added.

"You are coming with us," Hypnos said. "You're with us, and now you'll be with Gwen. That's pretty much the maximum amount of being with us. My dad is a prickly cuss who hates humans. Showing up with three of your kind is going to send him to the moon."

"What's wrong with humans?"

Hypnos wrinkled his nose. "You ever been around a pack of yappy, barking dogs?"

"Yes," Gwen said. "They're the worst."

Hypnos nodded. "That's what most gods think of you. Come now, Queen Rose. We have business to attend."

"Why does she get to go?" Bernadette asked.

Hypnos slammed the door closed. "Because I like her best."

I caught up with him when he paused at the curb. Gwen screamed something out the window as she sped away which I can only assume I was happy not to hear. "That wasn't nice."

"He would have killed them on sight," Hypnos said. "Especially Nimue."

"Nim—Wait! That girl is the Wicked Witch?"

"You didn't know?" He chuckled. "It's so obvious."

"I'm going to kill her!" I said, taking off toward the car. Hypnos grabbed me and pulled me back. "Let me go!"

Hypnos turned me toward the townhouse. "There will be time to get her later, but right now we have more important business."

"I can't believe she got back to Earth. How did she--?"

Hypnos sighed. "I can only imagine it had something to do with setting my brother free."

"She did that?" I fumed.

Hypnos blew a deep breath. "I'm not sure. It's only an assumption. I'm not omniscient, just a very good guesser. Plus, she has my brother's blessing embedded deep in her soul."

"I'm going to kill her."

"Please don't," Hypnos said, walking forward. "Murder is frowned upon in this plane, and if you kill her, she won't just explode into ashes. There will be blood and a big mess." He jogged up the steps to the door. "Now come on."

I couldn't believe it. My greatest enemy was driving away with my friend. I should text them. I should—I patted my pocket but found nothing. I had left my phone in Gwen's car. "Crud."

"This isn't the time!" Hypnos said. "Gwen can protect herself."

"And if she can't?"

Hypnos knocked on the door. "You're about to meet a god more powerful than almost any in the cosmos. He could kill you with just a thought, and you're worried about a petty squabble. Perspective, please."

It wasn't petty. She nearly killed me, and Chelle, and... yeah, okay, I didn't like her. But it wasn't something that I could tell Hypnos, who was laser focused on his goal, disregarding anything else or anyone else's feelings. I sighed and spun toward the door, meeting him at the top of the stairs. Hypnos's hands shook in fear. I took one of them and squeezed it tightly. "It's going to be okay."

"You don't know him."

I nodded. "Thank god. He sounds like the worst. I might not know him, but I know what it's like having terrible, overbearing parents that use terror to keep you in line."

"Mine are worse, I promise you that."

"It's not a competition, ok—"

"I'm not so bad." a gravelly voice said from behind the door. The door creaked open and a tall, thin man stepped into the light. When he smiled, everything around him electrified, making it feel a bit brighter and more vibrant. Only the shadow of his features could be seen in the bright light of day—the tip of a nose, the edge of a mouth, the white of his dark eyes. "Hypnos exaggerates all my faults, as he is known to do, and fails to acknowledge my many, many strengths."

"Hi, Dad," Hypnos said, losing all the confident stagger I had seen from him. He was like a nervous little child facing his mother after having broken a lamp.

"After ten thousand years, that's all you have to say to me?" Erebus said, disappointment oozing from his words.

Hypnos dropped his head. "I know you're not much of a talker."

"That is true." Erebus nodded. "I am a man of action. What we do means everything, which is why I so hate when you drop your head like that." He placed a black finger, shrouded in shadow, under Hypnos's chin, and raised it to meet his eyes. "That's better."

"Nice to meet you." I knew I should stay quiet, but the words flew out of my mouth before I could stop them.

Erebus turned to me. "Ah, yes, I smell Hypnos's blessing all over you. He does so enjoy handing it out to every mortal he meets."

"DAAAAAD!" Hypnos whined. "Please don't."

"I will never understand you." Erebus shook his head. "Giving your blessing is a gift, son, and you are judged by whom you give it to. Your brother knew that."

"He gave it to a murderer and genocidal maniac!" I screamed. "I'm way better than that."

Erebus turned to me and for a moment I thought I would be turned to dust, but then he smiled, and again, the whole world seemed to get brighter. "I like you. You have spirit."

"Thank...you?" I really hated when men talked to me like I was a child or looked at me like an object for them to admire. Erebus did both at the same time, zapping all my resolve.

"I got your letter," Hypnos said, trying to draw his father's eyes off me.

"Of course you did. Otherwise, you would have never been able to find me. Please, come in, let us talk over some tea. I make the best tea in the world. I should know—I've tried them all."

"No thanks, Dad," Hypnos said. "I just want the key. Can't you just give it to me?"

Erebus chuckled. "You know me better than that. You

are not ready to return to the Dream Realm. Your heart is filled with pain and malice. You wish to kill your brother."

"He stole everything from me!" Hypnos shouted. "Of course I intend to kill him."

"He didn't take everything," Erebus gestured to me. "He left you this lovely vessel to worship you."

I chuckled despite myself. It was hard for me not to be flattered by his words, as if they plumbed the very core of my soul. "I definitely do not worship him."

"Just give me the key," Hypnos said with a sigh. "I don't have time for your games."

"There is always time for games, my son." Erebus grinned. "We have nothing but time, after all. Urgency is a human construct. We work on the time of infinity."

Hypnos rolled his bright pink eyes. "I cannot deal with you for an eternity. What do I have to do? Let's get this over with."

Erebus leaned forward. "But I'm having such fun seeing you, and who knows when it will happen again?"

"You do."

"Not really. I only knew you would come eventually, but not when," Erebus said. "I'm not omniscient, just a good guesser. But I realize this is very unnerving to you, seeing me. Though I wish it were not this way. Very well. If you would like to get the key, then I need you to travel to Mount Olympus and retrieve the Jabberwocky of Antioch from your brother's room."

"Sounds dangerous," I said.

"It's stupid, is what it is!" Hypnos stared quizzically at his father. "Really? That's what you'll have me do?"

Erebus smiled. "Really. Return with it and I will help you further, but remember, the key will only open the door to the Spindle from the outside. You still need somebody inside the Dream Realm to open the other door from the inside, and only your mother possesses that key."

"One thing at a time, Dad," Hypnos grumbled. "Come on, Rose. We have work to do."

He stepped down the stairs. "Goodbye, Erebus."

"Goodbye, sweet child."

"He's the worst," Hypnos said.

"Yeah..." I liked him despite knowing how terrible he was, but I wasn't about to say that. I knew abusers could be very charming given the right situations. "So, when was he telling you about the Spindle, does he mean the Obsidian Spindle?"

Hypnos nodded. "Yes."

"But that's crazy. The Obsidian Spindle is in the Dream Realm."

Hypnos shook his head. "There is one in the Dream Realm, but there is also one here, and two doors block the passage from one place to another. One key in the realm of men, and one in the Dream Realm. If they're both used at the same time, the Spindle will open, and we will be able to reenter the Dream Realm."

I stood frozen to the spot, slack-jawed. I couldn't believe what I was hearing.

"Close your mouth. It's unbecoming." He shook his head. "Sorry. That's my father talking. He always gets to me. Come now, let's go find your friends. I could use a walk."

"You can't just drop a bombshell like that and expect me to act like it didn't happen."

"Weird," he replied with a smile. "Cuz I did, and I do. Thus is the burden of being a queen." He began walking away from the townhouse.

I called out after him. "How can you know where they are?"

"Please, I can smell my brother's blessing anywhere."

CHAPTER 15
AINE

"Don't be so glum," Epiales said as he bent to look inside my glass prison. "It could be much worse."

"How?" I grumbled. "This is the pits."

He leaned back on Loki's throne. "You could be dead. Or in the hold in the back of the temple with the other political prisoners." Epiales scratched at a chip on the armrest. "A pity. Loki did not take care of this seat. It's quite uncomfortable."

"What ever happened to Loki?" I asked.

"He feigned loyalty to the crown, much like you. He was all too happy with the old-world order, though, where Hypnos was gone, and he had free rein over this land. He failed to understand that Hypnos will not be gone forever."

"He won't?"

"Don't seem so happy about it. He's a jailer and an imbecile."

"You're a killer," I replied. "We all have our faults."

"Only to those who don't succumb to my will. If you submit willingly, then life under my rule can be very lucrative. Just ask your friend, Nimue."

I scowled. "Nimue was NOT my friend."

"Well, she did what I asked, and now look at her, safely back on Earth."

"She did it?" I asked. "She made it back to Earth?"

Epiales nodded. "Yes, and you could, too. All you have to do is bow to me—and soon, before I grow bored."

There was a flash of light in the room, and when it dissipated Agrona stood in front of Loki's throne. "It is done, my love. The resistance is done."

"Good. Good. And the portal?"

Agrona looked away. "The Djinn was released. The portal closed. I don't—I am sorry for failing you."

Epiales stood up. "Don't look so sad. We will find another way to open the portal, and then we will rule both realms, together, as it always should have been. We simply have to turn our attention to getting the Heart sooner than I imagined."

"You won't get away with this!" I shouted, but I had no idea if that was the truth. In fact, I feared that it was simply a lie that I was telling myself.

"Yes, we will. Hera is dead. Sekhmet is slaughtered. Hypnos is gone. The greatest warriors in the realm have been reduced to dust."

"Anansi is still out there, and the Land of Oz will never submit to you."

"That's rich." Epiales smiled down at me, then looked at Agrona. "Can you take me please to the battlefield?"

"Of course." She grabbed Epiales's hand and we vanished. When we reappeared, it was on the top of a sand dune, looking down upon a city of ash. Monsters roamed the bottom of the hill, and we passed them as we moved down the dune. "They await our orders."

"Have you found another way through the Wall of Itherium?"

Agrona nodded. "We have, your majesty, and we have breached the Gates of Droangor this very afternoon, meaning we have two contingents of monsters headed to the Emerald City right now."

"Wonderful. The Emerald City will be ours by nightfall. Let the monsters rampage. Turn your attention to the Heart, my dear. I will handle the Spindle myself."

"As you wish, your majesty."

"Meanwhile, pixie," Epiales said. "Look at what we have done to the strongest army in Urgu outside of Oz. We have decimated it. More than decimated it, we obliterated it."

The ash was thick as we walked through the crumbled walls and into the makeshift city. Soldiers screamed out for help, but none came. Instead, Agrona took her sword and stabbed it through the soldiers she passed, dusting them.

"They are no good for the rebellion now," Agrona said.

In the distance, at the center of the collapsed city, I saw someone I recognized, bound in chains. It was Boudica, the queen of the Mountain People.

"Why isn't she dead?" Epiales asked.

"She made a deal with the Djinn. I have tried to kill her, but to no avail. She is invincible. Must have been one of her wishes to not be able to die by my hand, or any I control."

"Interesting," Epiales said. "Well, I am not under your control."

"No, you are not. But I thought you might like to keep her. She set the Djinn free, which means she's our best chance at finding him again."

Epiales knelt in front of Boudica. "Fascinating. You set the Djinn free?"

Boudica didn't answer, except to spit on Epiales's shoes. Instead of sneering or hitting her, he laughed. "Yes, I think we would like to keep this one. Bring her to the dungeon. Kill the rest. Then, set out to the Heart. The journey will be perilous, but I trust you, Agrona. You are all I trust in this world."

"Of course."

And just like that, the Land of Oz became our only hope in the fight against Epiales. *Please, Anansi. Help them as best you can. Fight until the end.*

CHAPTER 16
NIMUE

I never tasted anything as delicious as a hamburger before. The juices dripped down my chin and I tried to slurp them back into my mouth so that I didn't miss one single moment of the bliss that was eating real food. I had just started to devour my second one since we sat down at a restaurant next to the water to wait for Hypnos and Rose.

"This is the best thing I've ever eaten," I said, still licking at the juices on my face. "In fact, it's the only thing I remember eating that had any taste in I don't know how long. The food where I'm from is...bland."

Gwen's eyes narrowed. "That is another very weird thing to say."

I wiped my mouth with a napkin. "It would not be if you knew my story."

"Any interest in sharing it with me?" Gwen asked.

I shook my head. "I'm not sure. It's circuitous and fantastical. I fear you will think me crazy if you hear it."

Gwen leaned forward. "Girl, every single one of these quests is crazy, and they're always crazy for different reasons. I'd love to hear it, but I'm totally not stressing, though. If you choose to tell me what you're all about, I'm all ears."

"Very well," I said, taking a leap of faith in trusting this new human even a single iota. "How much do you know about the Dream Realm?"

"Nothing. I have never been a quest girl for anyone from there before."

"A quest girl?"

Gwen leaned forward. "Yeah, you know how gods and monsters are lazy? Well, they always ask broken girls like me or Rose to do their dirty work, because they can't be bothered to do it themselves."

I nearly choked on my hamburger. "Oh my god. That absolutely sounds like them. And when you dare to defy them because what they are asking is ridiculous, suddenly you're the bad guy, and they smite you."

Gwen nodded. "Exactly."

"So why do you do it then?" I said through a mouthful of burger.

Gwen sighed. "I'm hopelessly addicted, I guess. I mean, it's something to do, right?"

I chewed thoughtfully and we were both quiet for a while. "No, that's not why I came back here. I came back so I could escape all that crap. Where I'm from, there's nothing but monsters and fairy tales and magic every-where. I just want to live a normal life and die a normal death. Maybe even end up in Heaven, or Valhalla. Nothing would make me happier."

"And yet you work at a pet shop with a demon and are now on a quest with a god."

I ripped another bite of the hamburger and swallowed it nearly whole. "None of that was in my control. I had to work with that stupid demon to get here. I just want to eat a sandwich in peace. I swear to you, I have no interest in causing drama."

"YOU!" I heard a shrill voice scream from the entrance. I whipped my head around to see Rose rushing up to me. "You are Nimue, aren't you?"

"Nooooooooo—" I drew out the syllable, stalling, until I looked over at Hypnos and he shook his head. The game was up. "I mean, yes, I am. I'm sorry for lying to you, but… well, my name doesn't have a very positive connotation, especially to you. I just want to—"

"I'll say it doesn't have a positive connotation!" Rose shouted. "You tried to kill me. You tried to kill Chelle. You— Chelle. Is she okay? What did you do to her?"

I shrugged, still clenching the burger. "Nothing. Last time I saw her she was trying to get into the Obsidian Spindle, and I let her go."

"I don't believe you. You were the queen. The Wicked Witch. You wanted power. You loved power. It was all you craved." Rose saw how much those words hurt me, and she reveled in them. "You are evil."

"Perhaps that was true there, and before, but not here, or now. All I wanted was the power to come back here."

Rose scoffed. "I still don't believe you."

"You don't have to believe me. It's the truth. I swear by every bit of my power that all I wanted to do was come back to Earth and lead a simple life. I just want to be sitting here, eating this burger." I took another bite. "Which is delicious. Do you want a bite?"

She shook her head. "No, I don't want a bite. I'm not going to take a bite from you. I should kill you."

I swallowed. "But you won't, because you're a good person."

She leaned forward. "And you aren't." Rose was fuming,

fumbling over her words, and shaking with rage. I would have been frightened if she wasn't so frail. "You're not coming with us anymore. I don't care what Etsop said. Come on, Gwen."

Gwen looked over at me. "Is that true? What you said? About leading a normal life."

I nodded as sincerely as I could muster. "I swear to all the gods in the cosmos."

Gwen nodded. "That does sound nice."

I swallowed my hamburger. "We don't have to play their game."

Gwen looked over at Hypnos. "I did what you asked. I need you to honor your deal to me. Save my boyfriend."

He looked away. "I—"

"You can't, can you?" Gwen said. "No, it's not that you can't but you won't."

"I'm on a quest right now, Gwen, and on a bit of a time crunch." Hypnos said. "I swear that I will do it by the end if—"

"If you get to string me along for just a little while longer?" Gwen shook her head. "No. Nimue is right. This is bull and I'm out."

Rose looked at Gwen, her eyes wide. "What are you talking about? He's going to do it. Hypnos is going to save your boyfriend. He just needs a little more time."

Gwen smiled at her. "You are so naïve. He'll string you along until he doesn't need you anymore, and then dump you."

"I don't believe that."

"Then you're an idiot, too."

Rose looked at me and then at Gwen. I think her heart broke a little seeing the two of us together but choked back her emotion. "Fine. Do whatever you want. See if I care."

She turned to Gwen. "I hope your boyfriend rots in that hospital—No, that's not true. He didn't do anything...but you're a bad person, Gwen." She turned to me. "And you— screw you."

She stormed out of the restaurant, and then Hypnos came up to us. "I need the orb back. You didn't give it to Etsop, and I have a feeling I'm going to need it."

Gwen squinted for a moment, then reached into her pocket and handed it to Hypnos. "That's all you have to say to me?"

"You've made your choice," Hypnos said, turning away. "So yes, it is."

Hypnos joined Rose outside. After they were gone, the diners went back to their meals, and I took another bite of the sandwich.

"Hey," Gwen said, taking a long pause. "Can I have a fry?"

All she wanted was a simple life, just like me. Perhaps together, we could find one, or make one.

"Sure."

CHAPTER 17
RED

It was hard to know if Cheshire was leading me into a trap because everything looked like a trap in the Mountain Realm. Even the plants had deadly teeth and a menacing glow. The closer we neared to the Wall of Itherium, the more monsters we found along our way. They seemed to be making a beeline toward a single point on the horizon just as they had with the battle line. We found encampments full of monsters, camp sites built and then hurriedly abandoned, along with the ever-present threat of monsters looming around every tree.

"I don't like this," I whispered to the cat as I hugged a tree and pulled him close. We crept through the forest at a snail's pace, lunging from one hiding spot to the next. Often, we were unwarranted in our caution. This time, smelled the rotten meat of a troll encampment, and their chatter floated on the wind as we neared them. We had to be careful, lest we be found.

While Cheshire could turn invisible, the rope around him could not, and thus he had to hide with me. I had no such camouflage, save for the amulet Sekhmet bestowed upon me that was supposed to keep me safe from all monsters during my travels. "I really don't like this."

"You shouldn't like it," Cheshire grumbled. "This is suicide for you."

I choked back a laugh. "If I had a shekel for every time I went on a suicide mission, I would be richer than the Queen of Oz by now."

"So, you admit to making impulsive choices and getting yourself into unnecessary trouble?"

"Necessary choices," I replied, steely-eyed. "And that often means taking necessary actions others won't take."

Cheshire popped his purple head out of invisibility and shook it slowly. "I wouldn't be proud of being a sacrificial lamb. Let's go."

He disappeared again and led me across a small encampment of trolls and back into darkness. When we were safe behind another large tree, I turned to him again. "Curious, trolls are not part of the Nightmare Realm. Why are they cavorting with your kind?"

"I don't know. If I had to guess, perhaps you've treated them terribly and they are ready for their revenge on the Land of Oz. Epiales has a way of twisting hatred for his own ends."

I couldn't deny that trolls were not the most well-liked of the monsters in Urgu. In fact, the Dream Realm had a habit of treating monsters as second, or even third-class citizens. I poked my head around the tree. I could see the Wall in the distance, but it was surrounded with the inky blackness of the Nightmare Realm monsters. "We're getting close. Come."

Cheshire hobbled from behind the tree. "Why you want to move closer to the monsters is beyond me. We should be going the other way."

"I must get through to the Land of Oz, and this is my best shot."

We traversed another clearing until we stood behind another large tree. In front of us, two onyx goblins fought over the charred remains of a rabbit. With them distracted, we rushed forward yet again.

"Can you let me go then, if you insist on being suicidal?" Cheshire said. "I brought you to the Wall. Look, right down there is the crack I told you about."

I craned my neck around the tree to look at the Wall of Itherium. It was big enough in my vision now that I could make out the blackness surrounding it. Dozens of massive, murky beasts smashed through a tiny crack in the Wall that grew bigger with each monster crashing through. They would be able to destroy the Emerald City easily with even a fraction of their numbers. Their army was impossibly large, and I couldn't fight through them if I tried.

"HELP!" I heard the screams from across the Wall, in a small camp a hundred feet from the crack in the Wall. I turned to see a young soldier, at least in features if not by age, screaming from the confines of a metal cage. "Help us!"

Five other men laid around the cages, out of energy to fight any more. A cadre of monsters surrounded them, taunting the men by throwing sticks and rocks at them.

"Soldiers," I mumbled. They all wore the green peacock of Nimue, even though she had been defeated some time ago. The look of the uniforms sank my stomach into my feet.

"I feel bad for them," Cheshire said. "They'll be ripped apart for sure, but not before those monsters have their fun."

"We have to save them."

Cheshire popped his head back in confusion. "That's going to cause a scene."

I looked back around the tree to the Wall. "Good. Then maybe we can make a scene and distract the monsters."

He crossed his arms. "So, you want to alert all these monsters to your presence, and then use that to rush through the crack in the Wall? You are an idiot."

"Do you have a better idea?" I asked.

"Well, yes, now that you ask," Cheshire said. "Literally any other plan. Like anything else, catapult over the stupid Wall. Find a magical spell. Use an amulet. Literally anything."

I stroked my chin with my free hand. "A catapult would likely kill us, and the Wall will prevent any mental ingress, except—"

And then a thought shot through my brain and my face lit up. I remembered, long ago, the Wicked Witch had used a portal to get through the Wall when we rescued Chelle from Hera. *How long ago had it been, and what had she told me? Think, Gabrielle. Think.*

After another moment it came to me. She told me that she set up portals throughout the kingdom as a magical way for her to do her business. *What did it look like?* A knotty tree stump alit as though fire burned through it. I remember, decades ago, seeing such a tree in these woods. I had avoided its magic then, as I didn't want the fire to spread to me. No matter how much I racked my brain, I couldn't think of where the tree might be.

"Cheshire," I asked. "Did you come across a tree stump that looked on fire in your journeys through the forest?"

"Yes, why?" he asked with reservation.

"Can you bring me to it?" I asked, eagerly.

"Oh no," Cheshire said. "That wasn't part of the deal. I was supposed to get you to the Wall, and that's what I did."

"Actually, our deal was for you to show me a way through the Wall." I thumbed over my shoulder at the soldiers by the Wall. "That is not, in actuality, a way through—not unless I want to be pulled apart. However, if you bring me to the tree stump, then I can get through this accursed Wall and you will be free of me."

"I do like the sound of that, but if I take you there, we're going alone, not with a group of soldiers. Get that rescue plan out of your head."

"We have to help them," I growled.

Cheshire shook his head. "If we help them, you die, maybe me too. If you want to save Oz, then you have to sacrifice them."

I grumbled. "Fine."

I looked back at the soldiers. *I'm sorry.*

Then, I followed Cheshire back through the woods and away from the Wall. I hoped the Emerald City could survive until I found my way to stop Epiales.

CHAPTER 18
BOUDICA

"Let go of me!" I screamed. Agrona was manhandling me through a temple deep in the woods, which reeked of sulfur and mold. Vines had long ago invaded and snaked across every surface.

"Shut up," Agrona snapped. "I may not be able to kill you, but that just means I can torture you for as long as I choose."

She squeezed my arm tight enough to show she was in charge, and I quieted down. There were few beings in Urgu I feared, but Agrona was one of them. I had watched her kill Sekhmet without breaking a sweat and had heard of her destroying Hera just as easily. She could not kill me, perhaps, but I feared what she would do if I flapped my gums too loosely. Besides, a warrior's best asset was the ability to sit and wait for their moment. The gods were powerful, but they were cocky.

We snaked through decrepit hallways until we reached the back of the temple, where the hallway stopped at a dimly-lit room containing four small prison cells with rotten wood for beds. The wrought iron bars squealed as Agrona opened one and threw me inside.

"I hope the Djinn comes for you soon, or you will be in serious pain," Agrona said before she slammed the door and stormed off.

Little did she know that I couldn't call the genie. I had already used my wishes, like an idiot. I could have wished for anything, and instead of saving my people, or those of the Sandlands, I wished to save none but my own life, so now I would spend what little of it I had left being tortured by the god of war.

"You must be powerful," a meek male voice called from the darkness. "To wind up in here."

"Who said that?"

"A friend...I hope," the voice replied, timidly. "This used to be my temple, my home, and my sanctuary, before Epiales came and promised me the world."

"What is your name?" I was tightlipped until I learned more about my captor.

A shadow moved in the darkened cell across from me. "I am the monster of monsters, they used to call me. Loki is my name."

"Loki is a trickster," I said in a huff. "If you be he, then show yourself."

A meek man crawled into the light. He could barely stand and quivered in the act of moving just a few inches. His skin was pasty, and he was missing several teeth. A welt over his left eye forced it closed.

"My gods," I said. "What have they done to you?"

Loki coughed. "I pledged my allegiance to them. They promised me a good life, a new world to conquer, and freedom. I gave them everything, but even then, they did not trust me. They knew me by reputation and saw every move

I made as a deception against them. They turned on me and left me here to rot."

"How have they forced you into such a miserable state?" I asked.

"They demand more and more power," Loki held up his hand. Three of the fingers on his right hand were cut from the first joint. Only the pointer and thumb remained. "They are hungry for it, especially Agrona, but Epiales even more so. His time in the cave made him yearn for power, the power of his brother, and the throne. There is something here in Urgu that he wants."

"What is it?"

Loki coughed. "The Heart—The Heart of Urgu, buried deep in the center of this place. It contains limitless power, and with it he can break out of this realm and rampage across the universe, taking revenge on the gods that wronged him."

"What is the Heart of Urgu?"

"It is how dreams are stored in Urgu. Every night Dreamers come to Urgu and deposit their dreams into the Heart and leave a drop of their essence. The Heart powers everything here. Hypnos's protective enchantments have weakened over time. If Epiales captures it, he will have every human's dreams from across the galaxy to fuel his rampage. He will slowly corrupt the Heart...as he has corrupted me."

"We can't let that happen," I growled.

"What choice do we have?" Loki asked sadly as he pulled at a thick iron collar around his neck. "This is a restraining collar powerful enough to hold a god. Nothing can break its grasp on me."

I shook my head. "No, something can. I just hope that he comes for me. A free Djinn has no reason to help me, except for the fact that I saved him once and gave his freedom to him."

"A Djinn?

"Yes," I replied. "He is pure power. I saw how Agrona looked at him. Even she feared the power of the Djinn."

Loki leaned back into the dark. "Then, let us hope that he does come for you. Pray on it with every fiber of your being. The Djinn are as narcissistic as gods. If you pray loud enough for long enough, he will hear you, and if you have a bond with him, then he will come."

"I have not prayed for a long time, god. None have proved worthy of my devotion, save my own people."

Loki nodded. "I understand, but perhaps, for your own life, you will try to do so again."

I sighed, crossing my legs in front of me and closing my eyes. "I suppose anything is worth trying once."

And then, I began to pray.

CHAPTER 19

ROSE

I was so angry I could barely think straight. Gwen had sided with Nimue, my mortal enemy, the woman who took Chelle away from me. It was such...bull! I wanted to scream, rail, cry, and rampage, but I still had a mission. I couldn't think too deeply about her betrayal until we finished. I pushed down my pain deep into the recesses of my soul where it could simmer until such a time as I could get my revenge. Then I would find Nimue and smash her into a wall, or, more likely, I would tell Chelle and she would do it.

Yeah, that's what I would do. I would tell Chelle, and she would take care of it, and then we would be together forever. Then, we could put this all behind us and just live.

Right now, I had a job to do with Hypnos. We needed to make it to Mount Olympus and recover the Jabberwocky of Antioch. It sounded like a fun adventure which would take my mind off all the crap I'd dealt with.

"Are you ready?" Hypnos asked. We were standing on the edge of a park in the middle of San Francisco. He put on his shades and grabbed my hand. He had no problem showing his magic to anybody that cared to look.

"I'm ready."

Hypnos nodded. "Then, let's away."

We flashed away. When we reappeared, I thought we would be on the storied Mount Olympus, which I'd heard stories about my whole life. Instead, we were back inside the casino in Reno where I'd found Hypnos just a couple days before.

"What are we doing here?" I said, breaking my grip on Hypnos. "This isn't Mount Olympus."

He shook his head. "No, it's not. And you're not going there with me, either. I can't risk it. You'll have to wait here with Jamil until I get back."

"What?" Of course, somebody else I cared about would betray me. What else was new? "Are you serious right now?"

Hypnos nodded slowly. "I'm sorry, but I can't just take a human to Mount Olympus. There are rules, and without an amu—it would kill you instantly."

"And why didn't you tell me this before?"

He shrugged. "I thought you would be with the one girl and the other girl, and it wouldn't be such a big deal, but now, well, everything's gone pear-shaped and I'm having to improvise. With any luck Jamil is still here and you can wait with her until I come back. It shouldn't take long."

"I'm not a little girl," I scoffed. "I'm not just waiting for you. I already waited for you with Mydnyte and I'm not going to do it again. I am a valued member of this team, dammit, and I demand to be treated like it."

"Would you rather die?"

"Kinda, yeah! Then at least I wouldn't be yanked around by you anymore."

"Trust me, you do not want to die. The underworld is in

complete disarray since—you know, I've said too much. Now, we need to find Jamil and then I can be off."

"Why even bother helping you?" I asked. "You don't care about me. You don't care about anybody. You just care about your stupid Dream Realm."

"Seriously? I'm literally trying to get back to the Dream Realm to save my whole world. This is not about you. It's about everybody in Urgu, including your girlfriend if I remember correctly. Don't you want to save her?"

"Yes." My lip lifted into a snarl. "Fine. Fine. You're right. Just go, then."

Hypnos walked into the casino. "Not until I know you're safe."

The hair of Apate around my neck allowed me to see the casino in all its glory. As I fumed at Hypnos and debated leaving him to fend for himself, a familiar voice called out behind me. "What are you doing here?"

I spun around and smiled when I saw Jamil, free of the amulet that made her look like a human and now in full wood dryad mode, complete with skin made of oak bark. No matter what I thought about Hypnos's plan, I was very excited to see my friend again. I wrapped my arms around her and squeezed. "Jamil! It's so good to see you."

She patted me on the back, and then pushed me away. "I wish I could say the same about you. What are you doing here?" Her voice was cold and distant.

"Why are you being so cold?" I said with a smile. "I thought you would be happy to see me. Is anyone happy to see me?"

Jamil looked around and then pulled me close. "You can't be here. It's not safe."

"What do you mean?" Hypnos said, spinning around.

"After you left, some real bad-looking monsters came looking for you." She looked over at Hypnos. "Both of you."

"Agents of my brother, likely."

"Possibly, or maybe another god with a stake in all this." Jamil shrugged. "I don't know who they were, but they looked like ten miles of bad road. I barely convinced them I didn't know where you were. They're still here looking around, figuring you would come back like idiots, and it looks like they were right."

"Where are they now?" Hypnos asked gruffly.

"Everywhere. I don't even know. You two have to get out of here."

"We can't," I said. "Hypnos is leaving me with a babysitter because—"

"Because why?" Jamil asked.

"I don't know if I should tell you if we're being hunted," I said. "But I can't go with Hypnos."

"You really need to not let Rose out of your sight," Jamil said, fear on her breath.

Hypnos shook his head. "There's a way, but it's going to cost a lot of money. A lot of money we don't have for an adventure that shouldn't take more than an hour."

"Well, she can't stay here. Neither of you can," Jamil said. "These are bad dudes and Rose is not built to mess with satyrs."

"Hey!" I shouted. "I could deal with satyrs if I wanted to."

"If I could, then I would." Hypnos sighed. "Honestly, I don't have the money to buy the protection we need."

Jamil smiled. "Well, if you need money. I can help you with that. I got hired to help put together a poker game upstairs. High rollers only. I can vouch for you."

Hypnos dropped his head. "I don't have the kind of money for that."

"Do you have that dream orb?" Jamil asked. "I'll bet it can get you in. The players are all about weird stuff like that."

"Is it safe?" I asked.

"No," Jamil said. "But the players are some of the most powerful creatures on Earth. They're the only reason I'm not pissing myself with Epiales' goon squad around. Nobody's going to mess with you with them around."

Hypnos thought for a moment, and then his shoulders slumped, resigned. "Then let's go."

CHAPTER 20
NIMUE

"So, level with me," Gwen said, gripping her steering wheel. "Were you a bad guy? Are you a bad guy? Am I hanging out with a bad guy?"

"I mean, does anybody think they are the bad guy?" I asked, looking out the window with fascination at the speed at which we traveled. I still couldn't believe I was free. "I don't think I was bad, just dedicated. I was doing what I had to do so I could get back to Earth. I would have made any deal and paid any price, but now that I am here, I don't think I am any worse than any other person."

"What's so great about Earth?" Gwen asked. "If Rose is to be believed, then you were quite the badass in Urgu. Weren't you a queen?"

"I was."

"So why settle for being a nothing on Earth? What's so great about being here?"

"Everything, my dear. In Urgu, the only thing I had to look forward to was the accumulation of power, but here, on Earth, I can look forward to every moment, every sensation. Have you ever stopped and listened to the blood pump through your body? It's truly superb."

Gwen shook her head. "That's weird, you're weird."

"What about you?" I asked. "If we're going to plumb the depths of our past, then what happened to your boyfriend?"

Gwen sighed. "I was on a quest, honestly kind of having the time of my life, and then everything went tits up. My best friend was killed. My boyfriend went crazy, and now… it doesn't matter."

"And Hypnos said he would help him?"

"Gods will say anything to make you help them. If nothing else, that's what I learned from all this—the gods do not care about you." She bit her lip. "Do you know what I got for that quest? The one that stripped me of everything I loved?"

I shook my head. "No. I don't."

Gwen's knuckles went white against the steering wheel and her voice quivered. "Enough money to buy this car. This crappy car that I hate is all I have to remember them by, and yet, there I was with Rose, doing it again."

"Why do you do it?"

"Because it's a drug, man. You need to feel needed. It feels good for your life to have purpose. You woke me up and reminded me that I don't have to do it. That no matter what, nothing is going to change, no matter what anybody says."

"Amen, sister."

A silence hung in the air for a moment before Gwen looked over at me. "So…where am I dropping you off?"

I shrugged. "Honestly, I have no idea. Anywhere and nowhere. I just like driving. I've never gone this fast on the ground before."

"I like driving, too," Gwen said with a smile. "Let's just drive for a while."

"Sounds lovely."

What are you doing? Etsop's voice boomed through my head. Every part of my body tingled with pain.

"Get out of my head," I mumbled to myself.

"What's that?" Gwen asked.

I gave you a quest. You owe me.

I pressed my hands to my head. "Leave me alone."

"Are you all right?" Gwen asked.

I dug my finger into my thick red hair. "It's fine. I just have a bit of a headache."

You ungrateful whelp. I have given you everything, and you turn your back on me.

I pressed my hands tighter against my head, but it was no use. He had direct access right into my brain.

Perhaps you do not realize that I can take away all I have given you. A demonstration is in order.

A pulsating pain coursed through my body, searing every inch of my bones so intensely I could do nothing but scream as tears fell down my face.

"What's happening?" Gwen shouted, swerving to the side of the road.

You are so enamored with your emotions and how much more you feel, but that goes for pain too.

"STOP! PLEASE!" I screamed.

Then you will do as I say, and never question me again, not until I release you. SWEAR IT!

"I swear!"

Good. As soon as the word was whispered to me, the pain subsided. Gobs of tears covered my face. I wiped them away with my sleeve.

"What happened?" Gwen asked.

"Nothing," I whispered. "Just a gift from Etsop, reminding me that I have a debt to fill."

She handed me a tissue from her center console. "Screw that demon."

I wiped my damp face with it. "I thought I could, but it seems...he really does own me, for a time at least."

Now that you understand, I have the address of a temple near your location which bears the mark of Erebus. Search it for clues to help Hypnos.

"Why are you so interested in helping him?" I mumbled through my sniffling.

That is not your concern.

He whispered an address to me, and I grabbed a scrap sheet of paper to write it down. Once it was written, I could feel a weight lift from me. It was Etsop leaving my mind.

"Are you okay?" Gwen asked.

I shook my head. "No, but I think I will be, eventually. I need your help."

Gwen sank back into her seat. "This doesn't sound good."

"It's not," I replied. "Have you ever been to Fresno, California?"

"Yeah, once. It's the stinky armpit of California."

"That's where Etsop wants me to go."

"Well, it's gonna suck." Gwen put the car into gear. "But let's go."

I took a deep breath. "Thank you. You really don't have to help me, though."

"Yes, I do. Nobody screws with my friends. Nobody. Not anymore."

CHAPTER 21

RED

"How much further?" I asked, following Cheshire through the woods.

"Just up ahead," he said, having turned visible once we were far enough away from the Wall and the monsters that lurked there. He motioned me forward.

In the center of a clearing a knotty stump glowed orange, pulsating like a heartbeat. "See, I told you I would bring you to it."

I held Cheshire's leash as I walked toward the tree. There wasn't any heat coming off the tree. It was all an illusion.

"Help me here," I said. "We need to find a knob to turn it on."

"No." Cheshire's leash pulled taut as I moved around the tree. He wasn't moving. Instead, he crossed his arms. "If you want my help, then let me go."

"This is not the—"

"Don't give me an excuse," Cheshire said. "This is the perfect time. You have gotten where you wanted to go—twice. I've more than fulfilled my bargain. Now, let me go."

I sighed. "You are not incorrect. I am a woman of my word." I sliced the rope with my knife, and it fell on the ground. "There you go."

"Wonderful," he said with a sly grin before smacking me across the clearing with his massive paw. I skidded through the underbrush and came to a stop under a tall oak tree. He licked his lips. "Now we can finish this. I am famished."

"Really?" I said, pushing to my feet. I pulled the daggers out of my belt. "You really want to go? I already beat you once."

Cheshire went invisible as he stalked me. "A fluke. Now, though, you die. And along with you, the last hope for Urgu."

He was no less lumbering in the woods than in the cottage. I heard every step he took through the leaves, and easily ducked to avoid his swipes. I rolled up behind him and sliced his back so that a thin trail of black blood spewed out and trickled down to the ground.

"You aren't invisible anymore, cat." I said with a smile.

Cheshire hissed into the air and charged, his blood belying his position. I spun to avoid him and stuck him in the side, implanting my blade deep and leaving it there as a marker. More blood oozed from the wound. The cat screeched. He had lost too much body fluid to stay completely invisible, but he wasn't clear to the naked eye. Instead, he looked like a piece of thin parchment held up to the light.

This time when he charged, I pulled three throwing daggers from my boot and flung them into his massive chest. The beast stumbled and crashed to the ground, wheezing.

"How?" he asked. "I've never—"

I pulled the knife out of his side. "Everybody has never been beaten, until they have. One day, I too will be beaten, but not today."

"Kill me quickly," Cheshire said.

I shook my head. "You aren't worth it. I will let you live with the shame that a human beat you twice, Cheshire, king of the cat beasts."

I moved toward the tree and felt around until I found a knotty knob in the back. When I pushed it, the light from the tree grew slightly and a portal appeared against the tree bark, emanating a bright white glow. In the growth of the light, the shadow of Cheshire stood and wobbled toward me again.

Stupid.

I spun and stuck him through the eye with my knife. Cheshire let out a howl and fell to the ground, his black blood seeping into the ground as his essence and form leaked out everywhere.

I wiped off my dagger on my red cape and placed it in my belt loop. Then, I stepped into the tree and the light enveloped me.

The portal brought me to the edge of a forest overlooking the Emerald City, where I could see a stream of monsters inching toward the skyline. I watched with a tear in my eye as fires consumed the city, the flames lifting hundreds of feet into the air.

Protecting the Emerald City would have to wait. My mission to entreat with the merpeople was all important, and if I were successful, the city would rise again, more beautiful, and more splendid than ever before. If the merpeople were not kind, though—no, I couldn't think like that.

CHAPTER 22

AINE

It's over. It's all over.

No. It couldn't be. All I needed to do was figure out how to get out of this prison, free Boudica, and get to Anansi. He would know what to do.

Why do I think he'll know what to do next? He was a prisoner just like us, trapped in Urgu instead of a glass case.

"What are you thinking, my petite?" Epiales cooed as he lifted me up from the edge of his throne and walked me down the ragged hall. Vines sprawled all over the walls and floors. The ambient purple light I gave off naturally lit the hallways as we walked.

"I was thinking about how we're all pretty much screwed," I said.

"I am not screwed." Epiales laughed. "And you are only in this predicament because you will not submit."

"That's not true!" I heard a male's voice scream as we neared the end of the hallway. "He's lying to you."

"Quiet, Loki," he grumbled. "You are such a fuss bucket. I should have killed you already."

"What's he talking about?" I asked as we neared the

end of the hallway. We were in a part of the castle I had never been before. A pair of rusted cells sat in the dark, with only a small hole in the far wall for light.

"Loki's always talking about something or another. He's just upset because I told him the truth and he doesn't believe it."

"I bowed before you," the voice said. A gaunt, pasty-faced man was squinting through the darkness. A welt over his left eye forced it closed, and several of his teeth were missing. "I submitted to you and you did this to me. You want nothing but domination."

Epiales leaned forward. "I want you to accept the truth."

"Your truth is a lie!" Loki screamed.

"It is not a lie," Epiales shouted. "When will you understand..."

"What are you talking about?" I asked. "What won't Loki understand?"

Epiales looked inside the cell as he spoke. "That he is no different than all of you. He is little more than a soul trapped here against his will. His immortal body is still out there, in the universe, being used by the gods like a mindless drone."

"My father would never do that to me," Loki said.

"And yet you believe he would trap you here."

Loki turned from Epiales. "He said I was a danger to myself and others. I believed him. I was headstrong. Once I am ready to join the pantheon, he will come for me."

"He will never come for you. You have to go to him and show him what a mistake he made."

"Like you will with your mother and father?" Loki asked. "This is nothing but a childish vendetta. We are gods. We are supposed to be better than that."

"You will see the truth. I will take control of the Heart, opening the door to the Dream Realm. I will reenter the world again and show them what a mistake they made for shunning me."

I couldn't believe my ears, but at the same time it made total sense. The gods in the Dream Realm were trapped here in soul and consciousness, but not in body, and if they could return to their bodies, then—

"Does that mean we could return to bodies?" I asked. "If we joined you?"

"Once I am in control of the Heart of Urgu, I can use the power to do anything. I can construct this world as I wish, manipulate it to my whims, open the door to the universe, and make the gods pay for their transgressions." He stopped and peered into my glass cell. "And yes, allow you to return to Earth."

Wonderful. Epiales had finally told me the crux of his plan, his true plan, and with it hopefully we could find a way to stop him. I had to tell Anansi the truth. I had to find a way to stop Epiales before he could control the Heart of Urgu, but first I had to escape my cage, if that was even possible.

"You are nothing," Loki said. "And you will be stopped."

Epiales hissed. "You will never learn. You are useless."

"At least I am not mad."

Epiales reached into the cell and grabbed Loki by the arm. Loki struggled against him, but it was no use. All he could do was scream as the color drained from his face. "Queen Aine, this is your moment. Show your loyalty. Give me the spell to destroy a god."

"I...can't. Besides, what does it matter? Agrona has killed a god before. Why do you need me?"

"She killed a god, yes, but not Hypnos. Hypnos will not

die easily, especially in this place. Only that spell will destroy him, and only you as queen of the fairies knows it."

Loki struggled, and for a moment Epiales took his eyes off my cage. With him distracted, I rocked back in his hand and pushed myself forward. I rolled on to the ground and the glass smashed around me.

"No!" Epiales shouted, but it was too late. He spun toward the hallway to prevent my escape and grabbed at me, forcing me to swerve and change directions. I pivoted left and flew into the cell across from Loki, just as Epiales snatched at me again.

"Pixie!" a voice shouted at me. I looked up to see Boudica, the warrior queen, thick with dirt and grime, and weary from battle, startled to see me. "What are you—"

"No time," I replied. If I left her there, she would be killed. She was a good fighter and would be helpful in the battles to come. "It's time to go."

Boudica nodded. "I'm ready."

"Then, let us away."

I placed my hand on hers and we vanished. We would go to the only place where I thought we could be safe: the Queen's Castle in Emerald City.

CHAPTER 23

ROSE

Hypnos, Jamil, and I rode the elevator upstairs to the penthouse of the casino, where a half dozen sinister monsters were waiting to play poker for money, respect, and magical objects. It seemed so stupid that they would even care about money if they could control the universe with their power, but that was the truth of the situation. Really, it was no less stupid than anything else that happened to me in the past year. Gwen said magic was stupid, and I couldn't argue with her. The more I delved into it, the stupider it became.

"When we get inside," Jamil said, looking at me. "Don't talk."

"Excuse me?" I said. "I'm not—"

"She's right," Hypnos added.

"I can't—" I replied in a huff. "I'm not a child. I'm sick of being nothing but window dressing to you people."

"Listen, it's not that," Jamil said. "These guys are crazy and powerful. If you talk, they are going to know you're a human, and they really hate humans."

"First off, I am not just a human. I am the Queen of the

Land of Oz. I have Hypnos's blessing running through my blood. I ruled over the Dream Realm."

"For about six seconds," Jamil said. "I just don't want you to die."

I folded my arms tightly across my chest. "I don't want to die either, but I also don't want to be treated like I'm incompetent. I ruled a gods-damned kingdom, and it was more than six seconds."

The elevator dinged and opened its doors to a penthouse decked out with gold and platinum. In the center of the room sat a leather poker table with nine chairs. Six of the seats were filled with beefy, exceedingly frightening monsters that narrowed their eyes at us when we entered. A Minotaur with a thick golden bull ring sneering at us. Next to it, a blue Banshee with green drool dripping down its chin and the black crown of a king. Next to the Banshee sat a gaunt monster with a long face and glowing eyes.

"That's a wendigo," Hypnos whispered to me. "In case you were confused. It will eat your soul if you let it."

"Thanks."

Next to the wendigo, an eight-foot serpent with spindly arms shuffled a deck of cards. It reminded me of the Basilisk from Harry Potter. Finally, there was a Centaur sitting beside a brawny woman with one eye—a Cyclops. Around them, a dozen other monsters, some lit on fire, or staring at us with cold, dead eyes, or sporting huge tusks, sat around drinking and waiting for the action to start.

"Hey!" Jamil shouted, walking to the table. "What did I say about touching the cards, Frank!" She ripped the cards from the Basilisk's hands. "Everyone, this is Hypnos. He's going to be joining us. I thought he'd make a good addition, since he's a god and all."

"Barely a god," the Minotaur grumbled.

"Does he have any money?" the Centaur asked. "Last I heard, the god of dreams was dead broke."

Hypnos reached into his pocket and pulled out the pink dream orb. "I offer this as my entry. A rare, one of a kind dream orb from the Dream Realm. How this got to Earth I have no idea, but I have not seen its equal in over a century."

Hypnos put the orb in the center of the table. The players all leaned forward to examine it. After several long, silent moments, the Cyclops looked up at Hypnos. "This is authentic and acceptable. Welcome to the game."

Hypnos sat down. "Thank you."

"What of the girl?" the Minotaur asked. "She reeks of human."

"She is my guest," Hypnos said. "I assume you will offer her the same courtesy as you do me."

"See that you do not touch anything in here," the Centaur said to me.

"Why?" I asked. "Is it dangerous or something?"

"No, I just don't like my room to reek of human."

"You know what," I said, stomping forward. "I am not just some idiot or child. In fact, that's not even Hypnos's orb to bet. It was given to me. It's mine, and if somebody's going to play with it, then it's gonna be me."

"Sit down, Rose." Hypnos's voice was a hiss. "You're making a scene."

"No, I'm not," I said. I was sick of being treated like I was inferior. "And if you're going to let him in the game, I demand to be let in, too."

"Rose!" Hypnos said.

The Centaur held up his hand to silence Hypnos, then spoke to me. "I like your spunk. Okay, we've never had a human play a game before. It should be good for a laugh, but you don't just get to come in for free. Somebody has to stake you, or you need a buy-in."

"I don't have anything…I'm broke and barely holding on to sanity here."

"What about your soul?" The Basilisk's tongue slithered as it spoke. "Has it been promised yet?"

"N-no," I said nervously.

The Minotaur pointed to Hypnos. "Not even to him?"

"No," I replied curtly. "My soul is my own."

"It is quite a prize," the Minotaur said.

I had something I could offer, but it terrified me to do so. My soul had only just been put back together, but I had to take some agency in this story. I made a decision, dumb as it might be, and hoped I knew what I was doing.

"Okay, I offer up my soul. Complete and unique. There is literally not one other like it in the whole world."

"Don't do this, Rose," Jamil said. "These guys play for keeps."

I sat down. I was sick of listening to them. "Is that acceptable?"

The snake slithered forward. "You offer it to us willingly, and for all time?"

"Once I die, yes. I'd like to keep it until then."

The Centaur laughed. "Very well, girl. I accept. You're in."

Hypnos looked at me. I had both disappointed and pissed him off at the same time. *Good.* I was sick of being his pet. Now, if he wanted me to help him, he'd have to play like he meant it.

"Deal," I said to Jamil, ice-eyed and bitter. She picked up the deck, shuffled one last time, and then dealt the cards. "The game is Texas Hold 'em. Rose, you're big blind."

A stack of blue and red chips appeared in front of me. I

saw what my soul was worth, and it was a fraction of what the others had. I gulped. Perhaps I had made a big mistake. Perhaps Hypnos and Jamil were right. Either way, I couldn't show any of them how scared I was, or that I felt any fear at all, no matter how much pumped through me.

"One blue chip will do it," Jamil said out of the side of her mouth.

I picked up a blue chip and threw it into the center. There was no turning back now.

CHAPTER 24

RED

I took my time getting down to the water behind the Emerald City which would lead me to the mermaid's domain. I had to avoid the throngs of monsters snaking toward Oz. I couldn't risk being found when I was so close to entreating with the mermaid queen for the key that Sekhmet needed to end the war. I managed to crawl down the jagged glass barrier protecting Oz from the water and set out to find a boat that would take me to the middle of the sea. From there I would plunge into the ocean and hope the mermaids didn't rip me to shreds.

SCHRREEEEEEEEEK!

The horrible noise sounded from overhead. An enormous dragon, black and dark, with bright red eyes, was staring down at me from thirty feet in the air. I had seen my share of dragons in my day, and I had never seen one like this.

Dragons were beautiful, majestic creatures. They were dangerous but they were not hideous, not usually. This dragon looked as though it had been eaten by darkness until it was nothing but a shell of itself in service to the dark lord of nightmares. Or perhaps it was a nightmare itself, a corruption of a true dragon.

"Easy, girl," I muttered, backing away from the shore.

The dragon shrieked again and unhinged its jaw, splashing black ooze out at me. I leapt out of the way and scrambled up the side of the glass barrier, away from the sand. By the time I reached the top, the dragon had flown closer and was ready to fire again. When it did, I bolted as fast as my legs could carry me, zigging and zagging across the field toward the only structure in the distance. The Emerald City.

A dragon was nothing to mess with and there was no way to outrun it on flat land. It was easier to fight them in the mountains where you could use the nooks and crannies of the land to your advantage. On flat land, your only hope was to find a cave that it couldn't enter, and hope that it lost interest before you starved to death.

Luckily, I had something better than a cave. I had a catacomb. The kings and queens of Oz all had the distinction of being buried in a crypt outside the city. It was one of Ozma's favorite hiding places when she was on the run from the Wicked Witch. It felt like an eternity ago when I had last been there, though it was probably only a couple months. Every day felt like an eternity now, and equally felt like it went by in the snap of a finger.

The dragon shrieked and fired more black bile down at me. I rolled out of the way and when I popped up, I noticed I had caught the attention of the squads of monsters hobbling toward the city. They ambled forward to fight me, too.

"Great," I breathed. "Just what I need."

I sprinted across the plain until I reached the back of the castle. The crypt had been covered over with a thin layer of dirt since it had been used to house Ozma, but its outline remained. I traced my hand along the O and Z ingrained in the door until my palm found the sleeping moon hidden behind a cloud. When I pushed it, the ground shook beneath me and the door collapsed open. I fell inside and pushed the doors closed, all while the dragon shrieked above me.

The doors would not hold long as the dragon's taloned claws smashed down upon them. The crypt was not built as a defensible position; it relied on secrecy for protection. My only choice was to make it further into the crypt before the dragon broke through the door. I stumbled down the stairs in the dark. When I reached the bottom, I felt for the shelves. Clay jars holding each ruler of Oz lined each wall, and they wobbled as my fingers passed them.

Another screech came from behind me, and the sound of wood snapping preceded the light now streaming into the crypt. The dragon was trying to push through, but the opening was too small, so it simply threw black bile down at me. As I ran deeper into the catacombs, I felt the thunder from above me. Epiales's monsters were coming. I had to get to safety quickly, if there was any left in the Emerald City. It appeared I would be able to enter the war for Oz after all, even if it was against my will.

I pushed my way through the dark corridors until I reached the back of the crypt. I felt along the wall of the tomb until I found what I was looking for: the moon seal. I grabbed the moon's nose and pushed hard. It stuck for a moment, but after another shove it gave. At that same moment, I heard monsters descending the stairs. I turned the nose counterclockwise and the door unlocked, sliding open enough so that I could dip inside.

Once I was through, I used the notch to seal the door

again, hoping against hope that the monsters were too stupid to realize how I had vanished. In the darkness, it was possible. As I raced toward the Emerald City, I heard the monsters barreling through the crypt, their thunderous steps shaking the very foundation of the tunnel in front of me.

CHAPTER 25
NIMUE

"You can't be serious," Gwen said, exasperated as she pulled into the parking lot of a gaudy, enormous replica of the Parthenon—at least I thought it was a replica. I was relatively sure I was not in Greece. Gwen and everyone else I had encountered spoke English.

"Forgive me," I said, crinkling my brow. "But we are not, in fact, in Greece, correct?"

Gwen shook her head. "No, we are assuredly not, but somebody clearly had a thing for it."

"A...thing?"

"You know, a hard on, or whatever."

"I do not know," I replied, cautiously. "But I would prefer not to find out."

"It's not—" Gwen pulled into a parking space and turned off the car. "Here in America we've only been a country for a couple hundred years, and we don't have a deep history...well, that's not true, Native Americans do have a deep history but we kind of kicked them off their land...but the white colonizers of this country took a lot from Greece when they founded this country since they had no history of their own, and that seeped into every part of our culture, down to the pioneers that settled the west. Generation after generation, more and more people had hard-ons for 'the old ways' which made many of them build these disgusting complexes all over the country as an homage to them, but they end up looking cheap and hollow."

"That sounds stupid. Why do you not just create your own culture?"

Gwen laughed. "America has a way of taking the easy way out of everything and building our own culture would have been difficult. If we survive this, I'll take you to Las Vegas and you can see the best and worst of America smashed into one place."

"No, thank you. I am starting to think America might not be for me."

Gwen opened the door to her car. "I think that might be the most American thing you could ever say."

I didn't understand why, but I was no longer interested in asking Gwen questions. Everything she told me made me hate my adopted country more, and I had barely seen any of it. I hoped when this was all over, I could see this place, and the whole world. Who knew, perhaps I would spend time in this Las Vegas as well.

I stepped out of the car and surveyed the different types of cars parked in the lot that wrapped around the building. Gwen told me that her car was "cheap, but efficient." The lot could easily fit hundreds of cars, and yet the lot was nearly empty. "What kind of car is that?" I pointed to a large vehicle with a short cab and long back, with wheels bigger than the entirety of Gwen's car.

"That is a truck. The owner is clearly compensating for something."

"What are they compensating for?" I asked, my interest piqued.

"A small penis, likely."

As we passed the car, I read a message adhered to the back: *My kid can beat up your honor roll student.* I paused. "Gwen, what is an honor roll?"

"When somebody does well in school, they are placed on the honor roll. It's the top, like, maybe 10 percent of a class as far as grades go."

"I see, and why would this child want to beat up the honor roll student?"

Gwen shook her head. "Because if you can't be smart, you can at least joyously display your ignorance. It's the American way."

I scrunched up my nose. "Where I come from, scholars are to be revered."

"That would be nice." Gwen snaked through the parking lot. "Come on, let's get this over with."

As we neared the replica of the Parthenon, I realized that the structure was not made from ancient rock, but a cheap façade that cracked and peeled across its face, revealing the poorly constructed brick underneath.

I pointed it out to Gwen. "Is that what you mean by replica?"

"Absolutely," Gwen said with an exasperated smile. "Lots of people call it *kitsch*, which is a nice way of saying 'we enjoy crap,' but that's America for you. Making the best out of a crappy situation."

We funneled around to the front of the structure, where a burly man in a tight-fitting shirt held a baton and stared at us grimly through sunglasses. He nodded as we passed. We walked up a long set of stairs, through some pillars and pushed open the tall oak doors and into...

....a shop, filled with people and different objects as far as the eye could see. It was much like the ancient agora of Greece, but with packaged goods instead of handmade ones. Along the top of the room were crudely-drawn paintings of the gods of old. In the center were Nox and Erebus, the gods of Night and Darkness, and their children splintering out from them, including Epiales and Hypnos on either side.

"This is—"

"America," Gwen snitted. I was going to say wonderful, but I let her continue. "If you can't make it gaudier and cheaper than the next guy, get out and make room for somebody else, cuz there's always somebody willing to make something worse and cheaper."

I picked up a glass orb with a reconstruction of the Parthenon inside it. "Fascinating."

"Let's try to find the manager, if we can."

As we wound our way through the tables, I brushed my fingers against the shirts that filled each display. One read: *Couldn't afford Greece so I took my wife here.* Another read: *I went to the Parthenon and all I got was this stupid t-shirt.* Others just had imagery of the Parthenon on it, but it couldn't have been the one in Greece, because there was a massive parking lot around it.

"Would people actually buy things from this place, even though it is only a 'cheap replica' as you said?"

"Hey!" a thin, bearded man said from behind the register. "We don't take kindly to that kind of talk in here."

"Cool it," Gwen whispered. "People don't like to admit their stuff is crap."

"Even if it is?"

"Especially if it is." She spun back around to the cashier behind the counter. "I'm so sorry. My friend is...

different, I guess is the right word. She is still learning the language."

"It's fine," the bearded man said in a huff. "You aren't the first and you won't be the last. We're just trying to get along. And hey, look around. People are happy and I bring joy into the world. So, who are you to judge?"

I looked around at the people speckling the store and it was true. They were laughing and joking around, many of them seemed completely comfortable being in on the joke. It was more joy than I had seen in decades in the Dream Realm.

"Very interesting," I said to the cashier. "I suppose that if you are not hurting anybody, and they seem happy, what is the harm?"

"Whatever," Gwen said before the cashier could say anything. "Can I talk to the manager or proprietor? I have a question for them."

The man stroked his beard down to the tip several inches below his chin. "Well, I'm both. We run a lean ship around here."

"Smart," Gwen said. "Well...here goes. This might sound really crazy, but does the name Erebus mean anything to you?"

"Course," the cashier said, gesturing around at the store. "He's kind of our patron saint around here."

"Erebus is a god," I scoffed. "Not a saint."

"Whatever," he said, but I watched his eyes when he talked, and noticed that his eyelids blinked horizontally as well as vertically.

"You're a chameleon," I said with a smile.

"You're crazy. First you insult my store, and now you're talking crazy. I'm going to ask you to leave now."

I walked forward. "Please, if you are in the employ of Erebus, we must know. He has a key—"

The cashier gripped my arm. As he growled at me, his eyes blinked twice horizontally. "I said leave, before you anger us."

"Us?" Gwen said. "Who's us?"

"SECURITY!" the cashier shouted and two burly guards came out of nowhere and descended on us. "Take these women out and make sure they never come back."

The guards grabbed me by the arms. "Wait! I'm not trying—"

"Enough!" he said. "Be thankful I am just kicking you out and not treating you in the old ways." As the guards dragged us out, he turned to the other patrons, who were all staring at us. "Nothing to see here, folks. Just a couple of shoplifters. For your trouble, everything is 10 percent off for the next thirty minutes!"

Putz.

CHAPTER 26

RED

The last time I'd been in the tunnel under the catacombs leading into the Emerald City, I was guiding Chelle and Balor into the city to save Rose and Ozma. *Ozma.* The last good Queen of Oz—of Urgu. The Wicked Witch dusted her by throwing her off the balcony. I swore vengeance, but never delivered. Perhaps one day I would meet the Wicked Witch again, and I would slay her as she slayed those whom I loved.

Finally, I reached the ladder that would take me up to the Cathedral of the Six next to the castle. The ground quaked as I white-knuckled the ladder and started to climb. At the top, I unlatched the trap door and peered out. Usually, a confessional blocked ingress into the church, but that had been demolished and I could see right through the ceiling, which was on fire.

I rushed onto the floor of the cathedral. The stained glass which once depicted the majesty of the Six in beautiful relief had been smashed and littered the ground, along with the stone that held up the ceiling. The roof had huge holes in it, some from great force and some from a fire that devoured the shingles like some hungry animal. The flames were making their way toward the great cathedral, which would be engulfed if the fire wasn't put out soon.

Huge screeches mixed with the cries of the citizens sprinting past the cathedral. Hideously deformed nightmare monsters swarmed the streets of the Emerald City. A small boy with shaggy blond hair tripped and fell at my feet as a throng of people rushed by. I picked him up and brushed debris from his jacket.

"Are you all right?" I asked the boy. He couldn't be more than six years old.

He nodded. "I think so."

I grabbed his hand. "Then let's hurry. Together."

Hand in hand, we ran toward the keep. We didn't get a hundred feet before he tripped again. I scooped him up in my arms and continued to run. The monsters were close behind, and two nasty looking dragons spat fire in their wake, destroying the tops of the buildings.

"Everybody inside the castle!" I recognized that deep brogue. Balor. Standing above the crowd with his shaggy red hair, he beckoned them forward.

"Balor!" I called out when I saw him.

"Good to see you, lass!" he shot back.

"The tunnel under the castle. Have you—"

"Destroyed," he said. "We would have destroyed the tunnel under the cathedral, but we wanted to give you a chance."

"Thank you, my friend." A screech behind me reminded me of the dragon coming up the street. As it tossed its fire, the people screamed and disappeared into dust. "You've done enough. We have to get inside."

"In a moment—" Balor said, hopping down from the light pole. "But first—"

Balor smashed into the ground behind the crowd. He was no longer a human, but a gigantic Cyclops, twenty feet tall. His changeling blood had never been more helpful. He rushed forward and smashed through a group of monsters, giving us longer to evacuate.

"Go!" he shouted to me.

But I couldn't leave Balor. I put down the boy. "Run to the castle."

He nodded as I pulled out my daggers and jumped into the fray, slashing through the monsters with everything I had, hoping that Sekhmet's charm would keep me safe. We fought off the monsters, letting more people evacuate behind us, until the pressure from the nightmares became too much. I turned back to watch the refugees streaming into the gate.

"We have to go."

"There are more citizens coming!" Balor said, pushing the monsters back. "We can't stop now."

He was right. On the other side of the castle entrance, more people were filing in. Just because he was right didn't mean he wasn't being foolish. The monsters stabbed and sliced at him, and even as an enormous Cyclops he was fading fast.

"It's one against a hundred!" I screamed. "We need you to survive for the good of everyone! Come on!"

"Fine!" Balor pushed back the monsters one last time before turning toward the castle. He rushed forward, and I followed him through the throngs of people trying to escape with us, and through the gates of the building. "Close the gates!"

"There's still people outside!" one of the guards said.

"It doesn't matter," I screamed. "If we don't close them

now then there will be no chance to stop the monsters from advancing."

Balor helped the soldiers push the gates closed as the sea of people crashed upon it. The screams of the people locked outside flooded the courtyard. I turned away from the carnage as the dragons tore down the street and the monsters rampaged after them.

"Come," Balor said, transforming back into his human-like form. The wounds inflicted on his Cyclops-self healed as his bushy red beard grew. "We'll be safe inside, the queen's protection is holding, but only barely. The monsters have realized they can destroy the façade without entering the building and they tear down the castle little by little."

He grabbed my arm as I fought back tears and pulled me along through the castle. A flash of purple light appeared in front of us. When it dissipated, Aine and Boudica were standing there, looking rattled.

"Boudica!" I shouted, wrapping her in a warm hug. "You are here."

"I did not expect to see you again, friend," Boudica replied. "What of your quest?"

"I am still on it," I replied. "But a dragon forced me off course, and here."

"Wonderful," Aine said, a snarky edge to her voice. "So everybody's messing up today. Can we finish the welcome inside, where we might be safe from these monsters, and Epiales?"

"Epiales," Balor said. "He comes?"

Aine nodded. "He is taking over the Emerald City and the Obsidian Spindle, himself." She paused and looked around. "Anansi? Is he here?"

"Inside," Balor said gruffly. "Let us hope the enchantments that protect this place can protect us from a god."

"I doubt it, which is why I need to see Anansi," Aine said. "Lead me to him. We have much to discuss."

"As you wish," Balor said and rushed inside. Boudica and I followed, leaving behind the chorus of screams filling the courtyard. The citizens outside who hadn't been as lucky were being dusted in the streets. Then again, maybe they were the lucky ones. At least their battle was over. I feared ours was just beginning.

CHAPTER 27

ROSE

Turned out I was actually pretty good at poker. Either that or the monsters I was playing with were garbage. Chelle went through a phase where she was obsessed with Phil Ivey and Daniel Negreanu. She watched their old games, listened to their lectures and classes, and even took a class on probability and statistics so she could figure out how to play poker better.

Or course, it wasn't about poker, in the end. She was trying to figure out how to bluff people so that they didn't immediately figure out she was a monster, and poker was a masterclass in deception tactics and subterfuge. Chelle never really understood the data part of it. I did, and that's the thing that I found fascinating about poker. I didn't really care about the players' physical tells, but I loved the idea that the cards had a statistical probability of winning and losing, and even a garbage hand could win depending on what the board showed and how you played.

Hypnos and I weren't playing together, but we had a friendly, unspoken agreement not to take chips from the other. We were, after all, playing for keeps. We already busted four players at the table, and they stood brooding around, bitter. The Minotaur was first, caught bluffing with pocket Twos against a straight to the Queen. Next to go was the Centaur, who went on tilt after losing on an Ace high flush to Hypnos's full house. He started playing every hand, even the garbage ones, until he lost the last of his money to me a couple of hands later.

The Cyclops was a good player, and I probably should have lost my all-in play to her, except that I picked up my straight on the last card to be turned over, while she just had three Jacks. A very lucky hand, but sometimes you need to be lucky in poker.

I also busted the wendigo, who was careless with its chips, and tried to bluff me with a pair of Sevens when I had a straight. Still, even with busting two players I was bleeding chips to the other players and barely holding on to my money. I got cocky one too many times and paid for it, so I was licking my wounds and trying to stay out of the way of Hypnos, who had the second biggest stack at the table, and the Banshee, who had the chip lead.

At this point, I didn't mind losing chips to Hypnos, but I tried to stay out of the way of the Banshee, who was clearly the best player at the table. The rest of them had a tell, but not the Banshee, who looked the same no matter the cards, slack-jawed, with green drool coming down her face.

"I'm out," I said, folding my hand. I didn't have the least chips, but I didn't have enough to bully around, especially when the Banshee was in the best spot to cash in and had the most money.

The Banshee didn't speak. She just pushed $30,000 in chips into the center of the table. *Was she trying to bully the pot, or did she have something?* I'm glad I didn't have to make the decision to stay in or go out.

Next to act was the Basilisk, who had the fewest chips at the table. If he lost, it would be hard to recover, which made his next move all the more surprising. "All in," the Basilisk said with a grin, pushing $90,000 in chips toward the center of the table with a sheepish grin.

"Too rich for me," Hypnos said, laying down his cards.

The Banshee moved her chips into the middle of the table and turned over a Queen and a Jack. The Basilisk turned over a pair of Kings. A slight advantage to the Basilisk.

"All right," Jamil said. "Two players to the flop."

She flipped over three cards. The flop was a third King, along with a Ten. The Basilisk pulled three of a kind, and was a big favorite now, but the Banshee had flopped an open-ended straight draw, which meant if it caught a Nine or an Ace in the last two cards, it would win and both kick the Basilisk off the table, and give the Banshee more chips than me and Hypnos combined.

"Fourth street," Jamil said, before burning a card and turning over a three for the fourth card, which wasn't a help to anybody.

"Come on," I said, crossing my fingers. I wanted the Basilisk to win to hurt the Banshee's chip lead.

Hypnos leaned over to me. "I had an Ace and a Nine."

That meant there was only one possible Nine and one possible Ace in the deck, which gave a very poor possibility for the Banshee to win.

"Last card," Jamil said. "The river."

She burned another card and flipped over the last card. The entire room, which had been waiting with bated breath, erupted. It was an Ace. The Banshee won, kicking the Basilisk off the table, and giving her a nearly insurmountable chip lead.

CHAPTER 28
AINE

Gone were the beautiful corridors that once lined the Queen's Castle. The paintings had been taken down and the furniture replaced with huddled masses of Dreamers. I passed the charred remains of the wall where I once saved Rose from an assassin. In the end, I could not save her. I wondered if I could save Urgu before Epiales's control was total.

I followed Balor through the hallways filled with crying people, dirty and alone. Many of us came to the Dream Realm without family, and never found their biological blood again. Still, we formed bonds with people, and as the decades turned into centuries, we found people we loved more than our families, and those we could depend on in any situation.

My fairies fluttered between the people, delivering water and checking on them. The Unseelie were once to be feared, but they showed up to help in Urgu's time of need. I was proud of them, and in our ability to put aside our feud with the humans.

Finally, after a dozen turns, we ended up in the throne room, where a statuesque Anansi, tall and regal with emeralds for eyes, stood around a cadre of my best soldiers, mixed with those from the mountains, with neon hair and bright eyes.

"Have they breached the Wall of Itherium?" Anansi asked.

"They have, in the Mountain Realm. They come from the east." A woman with bright red hair and purple eyes nodded. "They also broke through the Gates of Droangor earlier today and have ravaged the land with little effort. We have already been overrun from the east, and they will arrive from the south soon."

"What does soon mean?" Anansi asked.

A yellow pixie, a private named Jurgen if I wasn't mistaken, chimed in. "They passed through the Enchanted Woods three hours ago. We tried our best to slow them down, but their numbers were too great, and ours too few."

Anansi turned to a man with electric blue streaks in his hair and black marks running down his face. "Where are the monsters now?"

"They have made it through to K'dech and have burned the Happy Dragon to the ground yet again. They seem to be gaining speed the closer they come to the city. Worse, the closer they come to the city, the more their numbers grow —citizens with a grudge against the city are joining up. Dragons, trolls, orcs, ogres."

"Thank you." Anansi nodded before waving his hand to dismiss his troops. He walked over to me. "Please tell me you have some good news."

I shook my head. "I wish I did. I was hoping you would have found a way to fortify the castle from Epiales."

Anansi let out a deep sigh. "We have done all we can. Rose's spell to protect this place from any that would do it harm has held so far, but the castle's structural integrity is failing. We have nowhere else to go."

"No, we have the Spindle. It can survive an attack by a god."

"We weren't able to find the spell Nimue used to open it, so the Spindle has remained closed to us."

I blinked a few times and exhaled loudly. "What have you been doing, then? Because it seems like you've just been farting around here waiting for me to show up."

"I have been entreating with the mermaids on behalf of the Red Rider. I thought perhaps Nox would speak with me, and listen to reason, but alas, even now at the end, the old rules are still in place."

"What old rules?"

"We are prisoners here, the gods. But humans are Hypnos's guests, which means they can parlay in ways we cannot, even now, when all hope is lost."

"All hope is not lost," I said with as much confidence as I could muster.

"Let us hope the Fates see it that way. Our last chance is to barricade ourselves inside the Spindle as Urgu burns around us."

"I don't know why the door to the Spindle is still closed," I said. "Things haven't gotten hard enough yet? They have to let us in. We are the last of the Land of Oz, and the Fates are citizens of this place, just like us."

"Perhaps you can bargain with them. I have gotten nowhere."

"Bring all the refugees into the throne room. We need to make this quick if we can get the Obsidian Spindle open."

"Do you think there's a chance?" Anansi asked.

"I don't think there's much of a chance for us at all, truth be told, but we have to act as if there is."

Anansi nodded and walked away, leaving me with Boudica, Balor, and Red. "I don't like any of you."

"Blunt," Boudica said. "I like it. I don't like you, either."

"That being said, we have to work together if we hope to survive."

"The monsters are infinite. How can we even hope—"

"They are not infinite," Boudica said. "We have stopped the portal from opening and destroyed much of their army."

"How?" Red asked.

Boudica smiled. "They were using the Djinn, and Sekhmet gave her life to save us and close the portal."

"Where is the Djinn now?" I asked.

"I don't know. I set it free and—"

"Set it free?" Balor said. "Are you mad? We fight for our lives and you *let it go*?"

"It was the only way it would help us!" Boudica shot back.

"Children!" I shouted and waited for them to quiet down. "This is good news. If you have touched the Djinn, then it is linked to you. You can call it again."

"I have tried many times. There's not—"

"That wasn't a question!" I snapped. "We don't have many cards left to play. If we have a Djinn in our corner, then we have to try to use it." I fluttered closer to Boudica. "Do what you can, okay?"

Boudica nodded. "Aye."

I turned to Red and Balor. "Meanwhile, you two help us get everybody into the throne room."

"Who made you queen?" Red said.

"I have been queen since Rose died," I said. "And I have

been a queen to my people for eons. If you have one more qualified, I would like to see them." Red and Balor didn't say anything. "I didn't think so. Please now, do as I say. We have to work together if we hope to survive."

It felt good to wield the power of the queen again. It almost sounded like I knew what I was doing.

CHAPTER 29

ROSE

The line to the bathroom in the penthouse poker suite was long, but the monsters let me cut to the front because I was in the game. I splashed water on my face. I didn't even know how long we had been playing. The sun had set across Reno, the lights of the city flickered in the hills outside of the penthouse window, and we hadn't gotten anywhere. The Banshee still had a 2:1 chip lead over both me and Hypnos. It felt like we were doing little more than exchanging the same money around the table.

It's a lot harder to play conservatively when competing with only three people. When there's more people in the game, the blinds move around the table and you aren't in almost every hand. You can also wait for a great hand. When it's only three people, a good hand might be a Jack and a Ten, something you would rarely play with a full table. However, since there were fewer hands in play at any one time, the odds that a crappy hand is going to win goes up.

There was a knock on the door and a sharp male voice

pierced through my thoughts. "Come on in there! Don't blow up the bathroom!"

I sighed. It was time to get back in the game. I could only take a one hand break every hour, and that only because I was a human. The Banshee and Hypnos felt no fatigue, and it was wearing on me.

I pushed open the door to see a cocky, clean-shaven man with a top hat and red velvet coat over a stained t-shirt. "Sorry, babe. I didn't mean to rush you, but I have to pee like Pegasus."

"Whatever."

"Come find me later, though," he said, sliding past me with a smile. "I'd love to hear all your secrets."

I walked past the throngs of monsters and sat down at the table next to Hypnos. The pot wasn't that big, but the Banshee was throwing her weight around. There was a Jack, Three, Seven, Nine, and Ace on the board.

"Call," Hypnos said, pushing in his chips. "Two pairs. Jacks and Threes."

The Banshee turned over her cards. Three Sevens. Two in her hand and one on the board. Hypnos grumbled as he watched her collect her winnings. "Good hand."

"This is taking forever," I said, cracking my neck. Every bone in my body was sore. "I didn't know you could get so sore sitting still, or so exhausted."

Jamil shuffled the cards and dealt again. "Bet is to you, Hypnos."

Hypnos looked down at his chips. "Fifty thousand raise." He pushed his chips into the pot. Hypnos and I weren't playing as a team, but we weren't playing against each other either, so I figured I would bow out of the hand...

...and then I turned over my hand and had a pair of Kings. Kings was a good hand for a nine-player game. It was dominant in a three player one. I had to go in. Between the two of us, we had a good chance of taking a lot of money from Banshee. It also meant that I would be going all in with my entire stack. I couldn't help it. I had to do it. "All in."

Hypnos and I exchanged a worried glance. It would be a good-sized hit to his stack, but it would cripple me to lose. And I was playing for my soul—my immortal soul.

Jamil looked at me. "You sure?"

I sighed, and pushed all my chips in. "You heard me."

The Banshee had played almost every hand for the last hour, and with both Hypnos and me reeling, I assumed she would go in if she had anything, as she was getting very good pot odds. However, after a long think, she folded her cards—leaving just Hypnos and I playing against each other, my soul on the line.

"What do you have?" Hypnos asked.

I turned over a pair of Kings and waited until Hypnos turned over a pair of tens. I was ahead and in great position to double up my chips, though I regretted it had to be at the Dream God's expense.

"Let's see the cards," Jamil said. She burned one card and flipped over three. A Jack, a Queen, and a Ten. A Ten gave Hypnos three of a kind. He was beating me, but it was okay. I had a lot of outs. I could catch an Ace, a Nine, or a third King.

"Next card," Jamil said, before burning a card and flipping over a Two. "No help to Rose."

One card. There was one card left...and my palms were sweating. Jamil burned the card, and then flipped over the next one.

"A Five," Jamil said, sadly. "Hypnos wins."

"I'm sorry," Hypnos said, dropping his head.

I smiled. "It's okay. It happens. Bad beat is all. Just...win now."

"I will," Hypnos said. "You can count on it."

I couldn't stay at the table without bursting into tears. Stupid, Rose. You wanted to prove that you were a somebody, that you could be helpful, that you weren't just a sidekick, and you ended up losing your soul in the process.

I pressed my hands against my chest, fearing that it would be taken from me at any moment. No, that wasn't how it worked. The deal I made meant my soul wouldn't be taken until I was dead, which meant I needed to survive as long as possible.

What were you thinking? If Chelle were here, she would smack me so hard. But she wasn't there, and remembering I couldn't call out to her brought a second wave of pain, and the tears came in spite of me. I didn't care if I looked strong or weak. Either way, I looked like an idiot.

CHAPTER 30
RED

"Get to the throne room!" I shouted to a group of refugees huddled near the front door of the castle. I had made my way through the hallways leading toward the front gate and out into the stables and cleared most of the refugees from the castle walls along the way. Several soldiers stabbed at the horde of monsters through gaps between the iron bars in the gate, while others braced themselves against it, grimacing and sweaty, to hold back the monsters from breaking it down. The gate was strong, built by magic and dwarven hands, but it could not withstand forever.

"Fools."

I heard the grumble from the sky, deeper than any voice I had ever heard before. The tone of it was so thunderous that it broke the windows of the building across from us and sent glass shattering into the courtyard. Soldiers dropped to their knees to cover their ears from the sound.

"Let us end this."

In front of me materialized a tall man with a shaggy beard and long, black hair. His eyes glistened in the way I had only seen in gods, and it didn't take me long to discern who he was. Epiales.

"Come no closer, vile god!" I shouted, pulling my daggers from their sheaths. I was under no delusion that I could fight the god, but I hoped the spell Rose had activated, which prevented any who wished to harm the people of Oz from entering, would keep him out. I kept my strength in that.

Epiales chuckled to himself. When he spoke, his voice no longer boomed through the sky, but it had lost none of its depth. "Silly child. You will submit to me or die."

"I think neither," I replied with a wry smile, my confidence fading with each step he took toward the castle. "You will regret it if you come closer."

"And who will be the bringer of this regret, you?" He answered his own question with another step, when the spell protecting the castle delivered a jolt through his body that sent him shooting backwards, crashing through the stables and sending the horses inside whinnying through the courtyard.

Perhaps he was dead, I thought, but a moment later my optimism was dashed when he rose from the ground and wiped the dirt from his brow. "Powerful magic, Hypnos. You have your tricks, that is for sure."

"As I said, you will regret it if you come closer!" I shouted.

"I'm sorry, my dear," Epiales said, stepping into the middle of the courtyard. "I cannot hear you up there. Perhaps you could come closer."

I smirked. "I think not. I'm very well protected in here and I would like to keep it that way."

"Yes, you are, aren't you?" Epiales shouted back. "Perhaps we can change that."

"How? You cannot step foot into this place."

"No," he said, aiming his hands toward the ground. "But I can send it tumbling down around you as the earth quakes, sending the castle to oblivion."

Epiales dropped his hands and the earth shook beneath him. The soldiers protecting the gate screamed as it collapsed, crushing them. The monsters it held back shrieked wickedly and streamed into the courtyard toward us.

A crackle of light and thunder ripped through the air, and Anansi stood in the courtyard. He held up his hands and the rumbling weakened. "You are not welcome here."

"Very brave, god," Epiales said. "Given what happened to your brethren. You can still join me. There is a place for a god of your caliber in my inner circle."

"Never," Anansi said, struggling to contain the quaking under him. His body shook more violently with every passing second until he dropped to his knees, unable to maintain his balance. His head dropped for a moment, but then it rose again, defiantly as he worked against Epiales's powerful magic.

"Are you sure?" Epiales asked, calmly, walking forward. Anansi couldn't fight against his encroachment and contain his magic at the same time. It was all he could do to prevent the earthquake from destroying the castle.

Anansi pushed his neck forward and sneered at Epiales. I had no idea where he found the strength to be so willful. "I will never join you."

His words cracked under the pressure of Epiales's magic, but his body stayed strong. Epiales took one more step forward until he was inches from Anansi's body.

"Very well." Epiales touched Anansi's forehead, and a burst of blue light ripped him in half. His body disintegrated into the ether, and I fought a tear from rolling down my cheek. "A pity."

The rumble intensified as it reached the door, and the columns that held up the front portico collapsed. I caught a last glimpse of Epiales grinning as the monsters streamed forward and the walls of the foyer crumbled all around me. Then, I turned and ran.

"GO!" I shouted to the soldiers and pixies still in the hallway. I took off in a sprint as the walls caved in. Thousands of years of history gone in a second. Soldiers ran along too, ahead of me and behind me, all of us hoping to find safety somewhere.

As I rushed past, a guard tripped over himself. I spun around to pick him up but before I could grab on to him, the castle's destruction ate him, and he fell into the abyss under it. I could not stop for another second. The marble was already slipping under me.

I turned and continued as the castle collapsed. The monsters snarled and I could hear them on my back, across the chasm. I had to admit, Epiales had a good plan. The castle could not prevent him from coming in if the castle did not exist.

I turned left then right then left, until I finally reached the throne room. Every fairy in the main hall glowed brightly, as well as the Mountain People's long hair, all of them working to counteract the spell. Their pained grimaces told me they could not hold off the power of a god for long.

At the other end of the room, Balor leapt forward as the dust plumed around him and another hallway collapsed. Monsters were coming for us, screaming and snarling, but as they moved into the throne room, they evaporated. That meant our defenses held, for now. The bottom line was that we were trapped like sitting ducks, with nowhere else to go...and Epiales knew it.

CHAPTER 31

AINE

Can't hold it for much longer. Even with the combined might of every fairy in my kingdom and the magic of the Mountain People, Epiales was too strong. My hands shook and my mind ached as I tried to control the combined magical might of the throne room. It had to protect us.

"How is it coming?" I screamed to Boudica. "Get through to that Djinn yet?"

She was failing miserably. The only power as strong as a god in Urgu was a Djinn, and apparently Boudica had freed one, which meant it had a bond with her.

"I'm trying!" Boudica shouted back, sweating bullets.

There was only one way out of the throne room, and Epiales knew it. We had to cross the Rainbow Bridge to the Obsidian Spindle, tame the hydra, and hope that the Fates would let us into their abode. They had kept the Spindle closed ever since allowing Chelle to enter but if she still lived behind that door, I hoped that she would be kind to us and let us in. She was our last hope.

"Where is Anansi?" I screamed at Red, who had just

rolled into the room. "He was holding most of this up by himself."

Red looking down. "Epiales...ripped him apart. He's...I don't even know."

My friend. My last friend left in the Dream Realm, after Rose was dusted. All I had left now were subjects, and even those—there were so few of them left. I wanted to cry, but it wasn't the time. I had work to do.

"We can't wait any longer to make our way to the Spindle," I said. "If we don't go now, we'll be surrounded."

"We're already surrounded," Balor shouted.

"Be ready," I said. "Once we break the spell, we won't have but a minute to get out of this room."

"We're ready," Red said. "Give us as long as you can to get the refugees to the door." She rushed to the door that led to the Obsidian Spindle, shouting for others to follow. The huddled masses made their way to her.

The force of Epiales's spell rocked me to and fro, choking the air from my lungs. "Go!" I screamed. The door to the Spindle opened and the refugees began to rush outside. "All of you!"

"But—" one of my fairies began to say.

"Do as I say. I am your queen."

There wasn't another word. The fairies and Mountain People rushed to the door. Their magic was lost to me, and I felt their powers leaving. On my own, I couldn't keep the place from collapsing.

I felt a cool hand on my shoulder. It was the soothsayer, the most powerful magician of the Mountain People. Her body was contained inside a porcelain vessel that resembled that of a human, but her soul existed in fragmented pieces inside of it. She and her apprentice, Shaina, stared at me with blank eyes.

"Go," she said.

"I can't—If I do, this place will collapse."

"We know," Shaina said.

They sat down and their vessels began to shake. "We cannot keep it up for long, but we will give you as much time as we can."

"You don't have to—Your life—"

"We have lived longer than we should have, and if we have to die to save our people, that is the best gift we could give."

"Thank you," I said.

Boudica stared at them, then at me, before nodding and rushing out. I broke my concentration and turned to the door. The soothsayer was powerful, but she was still only a human. She could not prevent the collapse of the throne room. At best, she would buy me seconds, but precious seconds they were.

The throne room began to rock back and forth and Epiales's spell overtook it. The soothsayer was able to abate the quaking until we made it to the back of the room, and I helped the last of us rush through the door. I took one last look back into the room and watched the soothsayer and her apprentice Shaina explode into a million pieces of dust as the ceiling collapsed upon them.

When they had vanished from this plane, the quaking intensified. There was nothing to hold it back. I turned to the door and fluttered outside, where a hundred refugees stared at me. They were terrified, stuck between a god who chased us and a hydra in front of us.

"While I tame the hydra, do what you can to keep the bridge from collapsing," I said to the Mountain People and the fairies.

If I was the rightful queen of Urgu, then I would be able

to subdue it. I fluttered across the bridge as fast as I could. The Mountain People and fairies chanted to help keep the bridge from disintegrating.

It wasn't long before the hydra noticed me. "Do you remember me?"

The hydra growled, but it did not attack as I walked across the bridge. Perhaps it recognized my scent, or maybe it had other things to deal with. "Sleep," I whispered to it, and it was all too happy to oblige.

"Come on!" I shouted, before turning to the door. "Open up!" I screamed. "Please open!" I tried the handle, but it was no use. It was locked. "Please, please! There are a hundred refugees out here. We must get in. Epiales is coming! He comes for u—"

The door creaked open and I tumbled inside. I fell to the ground and when I looked up at two haggard, old Gorgons stared back at me.

"It's about time," one of them said.

"You...knew we were coming."

"That you were coming, not when," the other said. "It must truly be the end time. I hope our help is enough."

"It has to be," the first one said, turning to me. "Go, get the rest of your people, and bring them here before Epiales reaches us and we must close the door forever."

I flew out the door to save my people. All of them.

CHAPTER 32
NIMUE

"This is stupid," Gwen mumbled. We were sitting in the car outside of the phony Parthenon waiting for the last of the customers to file out.

"I don't disagree with you," I said, staring intently at the front door. "But there is something going on in that stupid building, and I'm very sure that Etsop will not let me go until I figure it out. You don't have to be part of this." I glanced over at her. "In fact, I'm kind of surprised you're still around."

"Are you kidding me? I work in a diner, attached to a crappy hotel, across from a mechanic shop in the middle of nowhere. I may hate the gods, but this is the most fun I've had in months. Did you know you told off a god and his chosen one?"

I nodded. "I do. As you mentioned, I'm the one who did it. What of it?"

Gwen slammed her hands on the steering wheel. "It's bonkers is what it is. He could have blown your head off without a second thought, but you just don't give even one care! I wish I had those cajones. You're absolutely bonkers and I can't look away. What are we gonna find in there? Gold? A key to a magical land? A bag of noses? A trip to the police station? Who knows, but I kinda can't not find out."

"You're a bit of an adrenaline seeker, aren't you?"

Gwen shrugged. "Sure, but whatever. You're the consciousness of a dead queen implanted into the body of a hot redhead. We've all got our demons."

My eyebrows shot up. "You think I'm hot?"

"I mean, I'm not that into girls, but I can objectively say that Etsop has very good taste for a demon."

I felt my cheeks getting warm. "Thank you."

Gwen stared out the window, leaning closer as she watched somebody walk out of the building. "I think that's the owner, which means there's not any more people in there. I counted fifty-four people when we left, and ninety-seven more entered throughout the rest of the day. Between security and the owner, a hundred and sixty-four have exited. Those are all the people I saw when we were inside."

I stared at her with a newfound respect and a bit of awe. "You are spooky good at that."

She chuckled. "Well, it doesn't take a genius to be wrong."

We watched the manager walk to his car and drive away. There was a moment when I swore he spotted us, but he was only watching a deer hop into the woods. Once he turned away and was gone, we watched long enough to make sure there were no more security guards around. Finally, Gwen and I got out of the car and walked up to the front door.

"Wait," Gwen said, looking up at the door jamb. "That's weird. Doesn't seem to be any security on this door." She looked up. "No cameras, either."

"Perhaps there is nothing valuable to steal inside."

"Maybe, but it's still just really weird. Almost everywhere has a security camera now. Even my mom's house has one."

"Does that mean it's safe to enter?"

"I don't know," Gwen said. "I guess we should do it and figure out if it's safe later, huh?" She reached into her purse and pulled out a lockpick set. She placed the pick and the tumbler into the door and in a couple of seconds the door swung open.

"It's true," she said with a smirk. "I'm very good at that."

"I didn't say anything."

She pulled the door open. "My manager wouldn't give me a key to the guest rooms so after a double shift, I would pick a lock to an open room to get some sleep. Beat driving home."

The door creaked open and we walked inside. The moment we did I saw a flashlight's beam flicker from the back of the room.

"Somebody there?" a woman's voice said. "Ernie?"

"Crap," I whispered. "Security guard. I guess you were off in your count."

"Doesn't take a genius," she whispered back.

Gwen pulled me into a stack of clothes as the woman walked to the door. We weaved through the racks of clothing and books as the woman's flashlight chased after us. Every time it nearly found us, Gwen ducked out of the way and I followed, until finally the woman scratched her head and went out the front door.

"See anything unusual?" Gwen asked.

"I'm from a realm that hasn't even gotten into the Dark Ages yet. All of this is unusual to me."

"I mean...god unusual, not like, the future unusual."

I shrugged. "I have no idea." I studied the room until I saw the counter where the owner had accosted us earlier. There was something under the glass countertop. It looked like a map. "What about this?"

Gwen inched over to me and squinted. I looked closely as well. The page had "The Labyrinth" written over the top of it, but it looked like no map that I had ever seen before. Gwen reached under the glass and slid the map out. She ducked down again and tried to hold it up to the meager light behind the counter.

"This doesn't make any sense," Gwen said. "It looks like a kid's puzzle."

Above us, the flashlight roamed around, and a shadowy figure stepped in front of the counter. "You can come out now."

"That sounds like the manager," Gwen said. "This is not good. I guess we really are going to jail, then."

I grabbed the map and stuffed it in my pocket. "Not necessarily." I pushed myself to my feet with my hands over my head. Sure enough, when I turned to see the figure, it was the manager.

"You?" Gwen poked her head up as well, copying my posture. The manager shined the flashlight in both of our faces. "Both of you?"

"My apologies, but we thought my friend lost something, and the door was open, so we didn't see a problem in checking."

"Sorry," Gwen said. "I thought I lost my earring. Then I realized I don't wear earrings."

The manager grumbled. The security guard stepped forward. "Want me to call the police, Than?"

Than shook his head. "No, I have a feeling I know what this is about. My father sent you, didn't he?"

Gwen and I looked at each other, then she turned to Than. "Yes?"

"I knew it. You know, my brother has been free for just about a hundred years, but I always knew this day would come."

"Your...brother."

"Hypnos," he said. "My twin brother."

I squinted my eyes. "That makes you...Thanatos, god of death?"

Than scratched his beard. "Not so much anymore, though it was always more of a bureaucratic position than people made it out to be. I have minions for that ever since I opened this place." Thanatos placed his hands on his hips and looked around at the shop. "I'm quite proud of it, actually. Much more fun than bringing people to the River Styx. What says me father?"

"Your father...he...sends his regards?" Gwen said, slowly.

"Regards! After all I've done for him." Thanatos scoffed. "You know what, I don't care. I did what he said, and he'll be happy to know that his plans worked perfectly. Not one person has been able to pass my test in the hundreds of years since he gave me the key to hide."

"The key to hide?" Gwen said. "Do you mean the key to the Dream Realm?"

"Of course, the key to the Dream Rea—" Thanatos's face dropped as he suddenly had a realization. "Oh no. My father didn't send you, did he?"

I bit my lip. "Afraid not."

"Crap. Me and my big mout—" He pointed his finger at me. "You could have said something, you know. Dammit. Every time. What are you, monster hunters? Groupies? Hippies? Either way, you aren't getting through my maze."

"Look, we just need whatever you're keeping here so we can complete this stupid quest we're on," Gwen said.

"We are *not* on a quest!" I said from the corner of my mouth.

She spun around. "Then what would you call it?"

I held up my hands. "An...inconvenient adventure?"

"That's literally a quest."

Than turned and beckoned us to follow. "Come on, then. I suppose I'll show you to it."

"To what?" I asked.

"To the labyrinth. I guess I can take some comfort in knowing you'll be dead soon. Come on."

I did not want to die, but I did not want to piss off the demon Etsop, so I followed behind Thanatos until we reached a tapestry of a Minotaur. He pushed it aside and placed his hand on the wall. It glowed blue and slid open for him.

"Down this way."

"I don't like this," I mumbled.

"Yeah, it sucks every time," Gwen said, descending the stone stairs behind Thanatos. "But that's questing. At least if we die, this will all be over."

CHAPTER 33
BOUDICA

Please come. Please come. Please come. "Gods damn it, Djinn. Where are you?"

I had been praying to the Djinn for the better part of a day between Loki's Temple and the Emerald City and it was getting me nowhere except for cranky. If he didn't show up soon, I was as good as dead. We were all as good as dead.

"Let's go!" Aine said, falling out of the Obsidian Spindle. I did a double take. The door was open? I didn't realize she opened it. That gave us at least a fighting chance. "Hurry up!"

"Okay," I said. "Fairies, keep casting as hard as you can. Everybody who can't fly—over the bridge!"

The refugees from the Emerald City, my Mountain People, and Red rushed across the bridge, which rocked back and forth. The destruction of the castle and the land surrounding it caused massive shifting. The bridge was the only thing that still stood on the mainland, all due to the magic of the fairies, which was failing.

Aine zipped across the bridge from the Obsidian

Spindle and joined her people, glowing a bright purple. "Go across. We'll join you once you're safe."

I nodded and rushed across the bridge. Red took the refugees across the bridge and into the Spindle. Behind me, I heard the snarling of monsters closing the distance on us as they rushed through the throne room.

I was halfway across the bridge when there was a scream. The fairy queen shot past me and crashed into the Spindle, I turned over my shoulder to see Epiales materialize in front of his monsters. With one clasp of his fist he destroyed the remaining fairies. They turned to dust in his palms.

"Boudica!" I heard Red shout, before my stomach rose into my throat...and I began to fall.

The bridge collapsed under me and I fell and fell...but then, something caught me. The rocky bridge was being reconstructed beneath me. It rose back into the air, this time surrounded by a green glow. Once it settled into its place, the familiar voice of the Djinn greeted me.

"Boudica," he said, floating onto the bridge. "It's good to see you."

"About time," I said.

"Sorry for the delay," he said with a sheepish grin. "I had to consider if I wanted to help you. Now that I am a free Djinn, I get to make that decision. To fight, or to wait."

"And?"

"This is my adopted home," he said. "We fight, and we fight together."

I looked back over my shoulder and saw Red push the last of the refugees into the door, pick up Aine and lay her inside. Then, she did something I did not expect. She shut the door to the Spindle and ran toward us, daggers drawn.

"No!" I shouted. "Go!"

"Not without you," she said.

Epiales walked across the bridge, the monsters behind him, lapping up whatever dust remained from the fairies. "This is a very stupid decision."

"We know," I said with a smile. Behind me, the slumbering hydra rose into the air and slammed its feet against the ground of the bridge. With the hydra at our back, we attacked. I sliced at Epiales, and got in a good cut against his ribs, but the god didn't even flinch.

"Come back to me, Djinn," Epiales said, all his attention focused on the genie. "We still have a lot of work for you to do."

"I will never be a slave again."

"A pity." Epiales reached out his hand and grabbed the Djinn by his face. Red charged Epiales, but with one smack he tossed her over the side of the bridge and into the water below.

"Red!" I watched as she tumbled down into the water far below. I turned to the god and swiped at him again. "Leave him be!"

"Last chance, Djinn."

Through Epiales's fingers, the Djinn grit his teeth. "Never."

"Your loss."

Epiales crushed his fingers together, and with them, the Djinn's head ground to a pulp. He tossed it back to his monsters behind him, as I watched Agrona with her white eyes come forward from the horde of them. With the Djinn dead, the bridge gave out, and again I fell. I looked up to see Epiales sneer at me as I fell into the water.

My fall was enough for him, but not for Agrona, who reached behind her and pulled out a great bow. Now that the Djinn was dead, his protection on me had fallen. Agrona could claim her prize, great hunter that she was, and finish her hunt for me.

She pulled back the string and fired two arrows into my chest. Every inch of me burned as I felt myself fading from memory. I looked down at my hands as they evaporated into the ether.

It was a good death. A noble death. A warrior's death.

CHAPTER 34
RED

I fell, and fell, and fell, watching as the bridge collapsed above me. I smashed against the water and it might as well have been brick. As I faded into the nothingness, I felt my head fall until I hit the water.

Then, there was nothing.

Nothing.

Just the depth of the water.

And the cold.

I thought I felt a thousand tiny hands reach out to me in the depths, but it might have been the last lie of my fragile mind.

Deceiving me one last time—

As I plunged into the abyss.

Ready to face eternity.

CHAPTER 35

ROSE

It took me a long time to pull myself together. I was standing on the balcony of the penthouse poker suite that overlooked all of Reno. The neon lights flickered in the night, sparkling like shimmering stars through my tears until the sadness dried out of me. I had fought so hard for my soul, first in the Dream Realm, then putting it back together, and now I had lost it trying to prove I was worth something.

"Cheer up, little pup." I turned to see the jerk who had banged on the bathroom door, adjusting his stupid top hat. Somehow, the shirt under his velvet jacket was more stained than it had been when I saw him just hours before.

I wiped the tears from my face. "What do you want?"

He shrugged. "Seemed like you could use a kind word or a warm shoulder."

"And you thought 'cheer up, little pup' were the words that would cheer me up?"

He smiled. "It got you to stop crying, so you got to give me some credit."

I spun back around toward the city. "I want to be alone."

"I understand that. I've had my share of bad beats in my life, but that was a tough one to watch, even for me." The man walked over to me. "But it's not all terrible, pup."

I glared at him, hoping he would spontaneously combust. "I just lost my soul, my eternal soul, for all eternity. I think I have the right to be a little bitter about it for a few minutes."

"I've heard worse."

I sighed. "I doubt that, but just for kicks, tell me. What would be worse?"

He readjusted his top hat. "Oh, I don't tell my secrets. Not unless somebody pays me a lot of money, and you don't have any left, do you, lil' pup?"

I balled up my fists. "Stop calling me that, and I didn't say to tell me a secret. God, you are so annoying."

He brushed his lapel. "Well, all I have are secrets. That's kind of my thing."

"What are you, god of secrets or something?" I asked, rolling my eyes.

"Exactly that, lil pup," he said with a flourished bow. "Harpocrates, but you can call me Harpo."

"That's the name of my least favorite Marx Brother."

He held out his hand, and I shook it. His skin was clammy and his grip weak. My father told me never to trust somebody with a weak handshake, and while I tried to purge everything my father ever told me, I still believed that deep down in my soul.

My lip curled. "And you are definitely my least favorite god."

"Do you know why I love secrets?" Harpo said, changing subjects as he looked out over Reno with me. He didn't wait for me to answer. "They have little value, except to the person telling them. But there is a cost to the giver. The more intimate the secret, the more it costs them to tell it. Because of that, secrets are very valuable to me, as a little piece of soul is wrapped up in every little one."

"I'll make a note of it. Too bad I just sold my soul."

"See that you do, because I know what you seek." He reached into his pocket and pulled out a red ribbon with a tiny metal medallion wrapped around it. "And I just happen to have a way to get you into Mount Olympus, for the right secret."

"How could you—"

"Please, that secret was written all over your face."

"I'll take my chances with Hypnos," I said. "If he wins, then—"

Harpo scoffed. "Haven't you heard? He's in a big pot right now. It will all be over soon."

I didn't do Harpo the courtesy of saying goodbye, I just gave him a shove as I moved past him and off of the balcony. I pushed through the gathering horde around the poker table, weaseling through their ranks until I was standing across the table from Hypnos, next to Jamil as she nervously tapped the deck of cards. The pot was stacked high, and there were two Aces and a King on the board.

"Who's ahead?" I whispered to Jamil.

"I dunno," Jamil said. "If I had to guess, the Banshee."

I could not have the Banshee win my soul. I knew what a Banshee would do with it, and I had no interest in being tortured for the rest of my existence. At least with Hypnos I would be with him in the Dream Realm, I hoped, which wasn't the worst sentence in the world, especially if Chelle agreed to stay in the Dream Realm with me.

"Bet to you, Hypnos," Jamil said.

Hypnos sighed. "$25,000."

The Banshee didn't say anything but pushed $50,000 in chips into the center of the table.

"Raise to you, Hypnos," Jamil said.

Hypnos thought for a minute, but eventually relented and pushed enough chips in the center to match the Banshee.

Jamil burned a card and turned over a seven. I couldn't imagine that helped either person in the hand.

"Another $50,000." Hypnos said, looking up at me, his eyes screaming his bluff. I knew then that he didn't have the cards, but he only flashed his truth to me for a second before stoicism washed back across his face.

The Banshee didn't think twice before raising it again, this time to $100,000.

"You don't have it," Hypnos said. "You don't have it because I have it. I don't know what you have, but I will make a deal with you."

The Banshee leaned in. Hypnos looked up at me and then back to the table. "I will lay down this hand, give you a commanding lead, if you give me back Rose's soul. It can't be worth much to you, but it is worth an awful lot to her."

"Don't do it, Hyp—" I started, but Hypnos held up his hand.

"I know what you're thinking...why would I give up if I were winning? Wouldn't you just want to see the cards if you're so confident? I get that, I do, but a little piece of you fears that I do have it. I know you don't have it. And the rest of your soul knows that if you win this pot, you'll win everything. There's almost no way I can come back from that kind of chip lead. You'd get everything else, except for one little soul. I'm willing to risk everything for the return of that one little thing."

The Banshee thought for a moment and nodded. Hypnos laid down his cards, and his only chance of winning, for me. He had won my soul, and I trusted him to be gentle with it, or at least more gentle than the Banshee. I wanted to cry again, not out of sadness, but out of thankfulness. The Banshee pulled her chips across the table, leaving almost nothing for Hypnos to play.

Hypnos looked at me and smiled. "All I have to do is double up a couple dozen more times now."

I looked over at Harpo sitting on a plush velvet couch in the corner. He patted the seat next to him and beckoned me to sit down. When I did, he wrapped his arm around me, and it took everything in my power not to wretch. His stench was foul, like a dog who just went dumpster diving during a torrential rainstorm.

"Did you rethink my offer?" he asked with a smile.

I nodded. "I have a secret for you." I leaned in. "I am the rightful queen of the Land of Oz."

His back straightened and his eyebrows raised. "That is a very good secret, and for that I will give you two gifts." He pulled the necklace out of his pocket. "This is for you."

"And the second?" I asked.

He looked deep into my eyes. The universe seemed to swirl in his blue eyes. "Run."

The elevator opened and four satyrs with machine guns rushed into the room. "Where is the god of dreams?"

Hypnos fell to the ground just as I did. I crawled past a dozen feet and under the table to reach him. "Time to go to Mount Olympus."

"We can't—We don't—" He stammered. "I have to take you to safety."

"No, we're going to Mount Olympus, and now," I replied.

"You'll die without that amulet, and I can't get one."

I held up the necklace. "I took care of it."

"How did you get that?" I said.

I smiled, placing it around my neck. "I have my ways."

He shrugged. "Then, I guess we're going."

Hypnos closed his eyes and my body felt like it shrank to the size of a pea, and then my stomach dropped to my shoes. All I saw was blackness, and I knew the next stop would be Mount Olympus. If I had to lose my soul to anything, I was glad it was Hypnos.

CHAPTER 36

AINE

All of my people, gone in an instant.

I was the queen of nothing now.

No, that's not true. I looked around at the masses huddled in the darkness, lit by the dim purple of my essence and the light from the hair and eyes of the Mountain People, along the candles the Fates held up behind them. *I am the queen of all of them.*

"I'm sorry," I said to them. "I have failed you. Our castle is destroyed. Our land is invaded. This is all that remains of the free Land of Oz."

Someone pounded on the door. "Let me in!" Epiales's booming voice spoke. "Let me in or I will send this whole place crashing down!"

My eyes grew wide. I spun back to the two aged Gorgons who lived inside the Spindle. "Could he—is it possible?"

"He is bluster," said one.

"Even Zeus could not destroy the Spindle," echoed the other. "It has always been and will always be."

"But the castle. I thought it would stand forever—"

"The Spindle does not exist only here, nor is it only protected by any one god," the first one said. "You are all scared, and the sight of a Gorgon does not breed comfort. I am Clotho." She turned her rail-thin arm to the other Gorgon. "This is my sister, Lachesis."

"And what of the third of you?" I said. "Atropos."

Lachesis dropped her head. "Gone, my sisters are. First one, and then the other."

"Gone where?"

Clotho narrowed his eyes. "The first, Atropos, died by the hand of the Wicked Witch, Nimue. Her replacement, Chelle of Earth, died to restart the Heart of Urgu."

I gasped. I had never liked Chelle, but the thought of her death brought a lump to my throat. So much death. I shook my head, putting this new information at the back of it. Instead I focused on the situation at hand. "The Heart beats again?"

Lachesis nodded. "It does. We feel its warmth with every breath. That is where we must go now, all of us."

I looked around at the masses of refugees, who had just survived a great ordeal. To ask them to move again would be cruel. "I will not make my people move without good reason."

Clotho held out her hands. "You are a good queen, but should Epiales reach the Heart before us and claim it for himself, he can destroy all of the Dream Realm."

"Or turn it to his twisted ways," Lachesis added.

I fluttered above my people, their petrified faces shaking as they followed my movements. "You said they would be safe here, that Epiales could not destroy the Spindle."

"If he takes possession of the Heart, then he will have control of all Urgu," Lachesis said. "While the Spindle would still exist, everything inside of it would be under his complete control, including all of your people."

"Then why would Chelle turn it back on?" I shouted.

Clotho stepped forward. "Because it was the only way to bring Hypnos back to this plane, and he is the only person who can defeat his brother."

"Hypnos lives?" I said, surprised.

"He does," Lachesis said. "And he fights even now to return to Urgu. We must give him time and hope we can keep Epiales at bay when he does."

"What does that mean?" I scoffed. "Why do you speak with such uncertainty? I thought you saw everything, the future, and the past."

Clotho grumbled. "There are some things that we can tell you, and some we cannot. Everything is going according to the grand design, but in order to continue on the victorious path, we must make it to the Heart, and we must leave now."

The Obsidian Spindle quaked. The monsters snarled and growled on the other side of the door. "This is the safest place in Urgu," I repeated to myself.

Clotho shook her head. "We will never be safe unless Epiales is defeated. Even now, Agrona works her way to the core. Hypnos's defenses have weakened over the eons, and Agrona is as strong as any god, save Epiales. If she makes it to the core before us, all will be lost."

I looked around at the frightened people. I knew what I had to do. "I ask too much of you, but you must trust these women, as I will, and let them lead us to safety in the Heart of Urgu." I turned back to the Gorgons. "I will not force them to go, but I will go with you, and I hope they will join."

Clotho nodded. "Then let us away."

The Gorgon made her way through the sea of people. Assorted cries rose up from the group as the monsters shook the foundation of the Spindle, rocking it back and forth. Clotho snaked her way to a wall under the stairs and pressed her hand against it, muttering something under her breath. A small door appeared, surrounded by snakes. Clotho turned her hand to it, and the snakes uncoiled and began to spin as their eyes glowed red. After a moment, a clicking sound came behind the door and it swung open.

"Come," Clotho said. "My sister will follow behind and make sure nobody gets left that wants to come."

I looked around, expecting nobody to join me, but one by one each of the refugees stood, the fear in their eyes turned to resolve. They would follow me, their queen, on our next quest, and I only hoped I could protect them better than I had the rest of their brethren.

CHAPTER 37

RED

I woke up in the depths of the sea gasping for air, struggling to breath, scratching and clawing at the water around me.

"Stop!" a squeaky voice said to me. "You aren't dying. Just breathe."

I jumped when I saw the horribly distorted face of a mermaid with its bright yellow eyes, green skin, and sharp fangs. But I did as I was told and breathed normally.

"Why is this working?" I asked, looking around. I was lying on a bed of coral. "And why can I talk?"

"Urgu is a construction of the mind. There is no actual breathing. It's all for show, as is everything in this place."

I wrinkled my brow. "Then why do mermaids not come up to land?"

The mermaid laughed. "Because you humans are crazy. It's much more peaceful here under the sea. Besides—" He pointed to his fins. "It's hard to walk with fins."

"Fair enough," I replied. "And who are you, friend?"

"They call me a name that you would not be able to pronounce, so please call me Eyo."

"How do you know English?"

"Remember what I said about construction and this place being a mind trip?"

"Yes?"

He jabbed the air with a stubby finger. "Bingo. Now, come on. We've been waiting for you. Anansi announced your imminent arrival days ago, and we thought perhaps you had died."

"No, I did not die. I was simply...delayed." I stood up from the coral bed and began to swim behind the mermaid. "I apologize."

"It is of no matter to us. There is a war going on up there. We were perfectly content not getting involved, though I assume that now you are here, that's an impossibility."

"I suppose so," I said. "Are you real, or a construction of some child's mind?"

Eyo shrugged. "I don't know. Some of us are constructions, some of us are real. We're not sure which are which, honestly. It's been so long since we've come to Urgu that it doesn't matter much."

"This is all so fascinating," I said. "And why do you pull people down into the depths if you are not hostile?"

Eyo had been swimming rapidly through the dark sea abyss but now he stopped and turned to face me. "Those people were drowning, or, more accurately, unaware they were not drowning. We were trying to help them. Some people didn't want our help, and most couldn't fathom that this was all in their mind. You must be smarter than most."

I shook my head. "I've just seen enough to roll with the punches."

We swam around an underwater mountain and a large, shimmering castle came into view. It was built from coral and lined with moss, but aside from that it had the construction of any castle I had been to in my life. We headed for the entrance. "The queen is wary of visitors, so be polite or she will kill you."

I smirked. "Just like every other monarch I had ever met." *Except for Ozma,* but I kept that to myself. "I think I can handle myself."

"Maybe on the surface." Eyo laughed, and bubbles plumed out of his mouth. "Those daggers won't do you much good, especially since you're much slower down here. More than that, it would be a dick thing to do to attack our queen."

"Fair enough and agreed."

Two mermaid guards, much larger and bulkier than Eyo, but with the same facial features and green skin, nodded as we passed through the gates and into the courtyard, which was covered across its top except for small holes that allowed water to flow in and out. The entirety of the interior was covered in algae, with fish swimming freely throughout.

A slender mermaid, stretched thin like a child's toy, waited in front of a closed door with a coral tablet in its hand. "François," Eyo said. "We have business with the queen. This is the girl Sekhmet sent, and whom Anansi championed."

"Name," François asked, looking down at his tablet.

"Belle," I replied.

"I don't see that name here—"

"Gabrielle," I replied. "Gabrielle Beaumont."

François's eyes popped open. "Ah yes, we expected you days ago. Please go in. The queen awaits you."

Bubbles plumed from the door as it opened into the antechamber. We swam through it into the throne room, lit by iridescent fish and algae along the walls. The throne room looked similar to every other that I had been around in my life, with pomp and circumstance and, of course, ego dripping off every pillar. Glow-in-the-dark algae ran down its center like a carpet, at the end of which were two raised chairs. A statuesque mermaid with a tall, glowing crown sat in one of them. Next to her, a woman—a human woman—sat with bright red hair and purple eyes, staring at us.

"Hello Eyo!" The girl said, sitting taller as we approached.

"Good evening, Princess Ariel," Eyo said in the kindest voice I had heard him muster. "It's a pleasure as always."

Ariel smiled. "And a pleasure to see you."

"Who is that?" I whispered.

"She is our princess. Ariel came here a long time ago and has since refused to leave, so we protect her. She says she likes it better here than the human realm on the surface, and we have never found a flaw in her logic."

"Eyo!" The queen's voice boomed. "What have you brought me today? More riffraff?"

Eyo shook his head. "No, your majesty. This is the Red Rider. Anansi arranged for her arrival some time ago."

"Ah yes," the queen replied. "You seek an audience with Nox, to parlay for a key she keeps hidden?"

I nodded. "I do, your majesty."

"I think it is a terrible idea for your kind to entreat with a god, especially Nox. She is mercurial and cruel and should have no reason to see you. She has agreed to do so, despite my strenuous objections."

"Why would you object?" I asked, trying to hide my disgust at her indifference. "If she is as powerful as you say, she should have no problem handling me."

"It is not her safety I am fearful for, but all of ours." The queen sounded bored, as though she had little interest even in the words she spoke. "Her emotions rest on the head of a pin. Should her whims fall in the wrong way, it could be the end of us all. Nox built this entire realm from an ember of light. We protect the realm from her unpredictable whims."

I shook my head slightly, careful to contain my movements. "I doubt she would want to have the Dream Realm destroyed altogether."

The queen sighed. "I am less sure of that, but we will allow you access to her. After all, you are, as you said, a very small speck in the stardust of the universe."

I furrowed my brow. "Is that why Anansi and Sekhmet sent me, instead of coming themselves?"

The queen nodded, slightly, deliberate in her movement. "Nox hates gods, but she has a soft spot for strong-willed human women, which you must be, as you have made it here against the objections of us all, and the universe at large. Goddess of the night, mother to Hypnos and Epiales, borne from the primordial ooze. From her mind the Dream Realm and Nightmare Realm sprung, among other things. Do not underestimate her."

I took a step toward the throne. "I will be careful, but if I do not see her soon, then Epiales will take control of this place, and who knows what he will do to it."

The queen looked straight into my eyes, her gaze piercing into the core of my soul. "I fear that this entire war exists simply to amuse the goddess of the night, but I hope you can entreat with her and save us all." The queen turned to Ariel. "Can you please lead her to the cave?"

"Yes, mother." Ariel kicked her legs and rose into the air. "Come with me."

CHAPTER 38
ROSE

Hypnos and I reappeared in the biting cold. We were so high as to be above the cloud line. No, not above the cloud line, but upon the cloud line. I thought I was mad for even having the thought, but my entire life was madness. After a trice of fear that I would fall straight through into the air, I realized that I was supported on the cloud, and didn't have to worry about sinking.

The thin, frigid air felt like daggers in my lungs. My knees shook from the cold, and barely kept me upright. The ground was loose and bouncy under me, and wet mist rose from every surface, obscuring my vision. I took a step forward and had trouble finding my balance. I fell to my knees and caught myself with my hands before I sunk into the cloud.

"Bounce," Hypnos said to me as he streamed through the air beside me.

I stared after him. "Excuse me?"

"You're walking on clouds. They aren't stable. Best to bounce, like a child."

"That doesn't make any sense."

"It doesn't have to make sense. It's magic." Hypnos sprang forward.

I flexed my knees and hopped into the air. Sure enough, my body bounced just like I was on a trampoline. I jumped higher into the air and when I landed, I rocketed myself forward with a big bounce, following behind Hypnos.

I expected Mount Olympus to be filled with gods, but it was deserted. "Where is everyone?"

"Moved on, mostly. Gods have houses all over the universe, and they don't spend much time on Earth."

"Why not?"

"It's small, and it smells funny." He stopped for a moment and I wondered if he was kidding. "I'm not joking. Plus, its most advanced creatures are psychotic apes. We legitimately thought you would have blown yourself up by now."

I bounced toward him. "Wait, so there is other intelligent life out there, for real?"

Hypnos suppressed a chuckle. "Oh yeah, much more intelligent than humans, but I still like you best, because your dreams are always so interesting. Most beings don't dream or dream only of simple things like what they saw that day. You humans have the incredible capacity to create and imagine things we never could have thought of when we designed you."

"Like what?"

"Like...the nuclear bomb for one. I mean, we knew about nuclear fusion, but we never would have thought to blow people up with it. In fact, you are all very concerned with blowing people up, much more than any species I have encountered."

I took a big bounce and when I came to a stop it was not on a cloud, but on a slab of marble. My knees shook to catch the impact. The mist cleared and I saw a set of stairs ascending up the side of a great mountain.

"Come now," Hypnos said with a smile.

I couldn't even see the top of the stairs. All I knew is that they were attached to the side of the mountain and twisted high enough that they disappeared into the sky above me. "So is this Mount Olympus?"

"Of course, though it's not in Greece. I'm afraid. The Greeks were very full of themselves to believe the world revolved around them. We're high up in the Swiss Alps, where no human could, or would, climb."

"Has anybody found it before?" I said, struggling already after only a few steps. "God, this is hard."

"You wanted to come, so stop complaining—and no, not that I recall. If they did, they would evaporate quite quickly at the sight of it, remember? That's why we needed to get you that amulet."

After several hours of climbing, my body was tired, and I was ready for a nap. Every part of me ached with fire, even my arms, which hadn't done much of anything except sway back and forth. Finally, when I could go no further, I collapsed on the stairs.

"Done?" Hypnos asked.

"So...tired."

"Well, get up," he said, propping me up. "We can't have you falling asleep. You'll die."

I tapped the medal from Harpocrates. "I thought this was going to keep me alive."

"It does, but you still have to breathe, and we've very short of oxygen up here." Hypnos pulled me to my feet and grabbed me under the armpits, lifting me into the air. "Better?"

"Kind of," I said. "My armpits hurt now though."

Hypnos clicked his tongue. "It's always something with you humans."

We climbed higher and higher until I saw the tip of the mountain. As we neared, I noticed high rise apartments made of glass poking into the air. Everything looked so modern, every bit New York City or Tokyo, but on a smaller scale. Dozens of shops and restaurants lined the streets.

"Not what I expected."

"What?" Hypnos said. "You expected us to live like the old Greeks forever? No way. You were created in our image, which means we have all the same proclivities to techno-logical advancement."

An angel with long white wings and a black toga shuf-fled up to Hypnos. "Sir, sir. Can I offer you our falafel special? Best on Olympus!"

"Don't listen to him," another, older angel said. "His food is crap. I can tell what you're looking for are some nice new threads to impress even the most discerning gods, and we have the best in the cosmos."

"Please, no," Hypnos said, grabbing my hand. "Let's go."

Angels shouted to Hypnos as he passed, all but begging him for business. Finally, we reached a dark black skyrise with bright orange trim. Hypnos placed his fingers on the keypad and the door swung open. We walked inside and the doors closed on two angels trying to sell us discounted sunglasses.

"That was annoying."

"Get used to it. If you hang around gods, there is a lot to be annoyed about all the time. Everybody is trying to get a piece of you. It's exhausting."

"That sounds horrible."

He shrugged as he hit the button for the elevator. "It's

hard to complain. Infinite cosmic body, after all, but it does have its downsides."

The doors opened for us and Hypnos pushed the third-floor button. When the doors opened again, we walked out into a huge flat, filled with multiple fountains, a dozen rooms, a huge kitchen, and about every amenity you could imagine.

"Home sweet home," he said. "Or one of many."

"You grew up here?" I asked, awestruck.

"Here and there. As I said, we mostly didn't come to Earth, but Epiales had an affinity for this place, just like I did. He really, really liked humans. It killed him when Mom forced him to control the Nightmare Realm. He knew humanity would see him as a monster, and they did. It broke him."

"She forced him?" I asked.

"We didn't have a choice in the matter." Hypnos moved down a long hallway. "Come on."

The hallway was filled with pictures of gods and monsters, but none of Hypnos or his brother. In fact, there were no photos of the family in the entire house as far as I could see.

"What did you guys look like as kids?" I asked. "Do you have a photo album?"

Hypnos pushed open a door in the center of the hall-way. "No."

I followed him inside the room. The walls were bright blue and lined with pictures of monster hunters like Perseus, Hercules, Lucifer, and Michael. Mixed with the posters were shelves filled with stuffed animals and books about every subject. In the center of the room was a bed shaped like a chariot.

"When did you live here?" I asked.

"We were very young. Mom and Dad gave us our assignments soon afterward, and we haven't been back since."

"Assignments?"

"I am trying to stop your brain from imploding by parsing this all out slowly, but I can see you will not stop asking questions." Hypnos turned around. "So, I will tell you a very little bit about being a god. If I tell you too much, your head will literally explode, so if your head starts to hurt, please tell me to stop, okay?"

"Okay."

"You know how there are gods of light and dark, and the sun, and potatoes, and just about every little thing, right?"

"Yeah, kind of."

"Well, there are those and many, many more, and those stupid assignments to protect this or be the patron for that, they are given by Zeus and the other primordial gods, like my parents. Being the gods of darkness and the night, Zeus gave them a lot of very dark things to manage, and when we were ready, they were given to us. To my twin brother Thanatos, Death. My brother Epiales was given the Nightmare Realm but he long coveted the Dream Realm I inherited. He spent many years lost in Urgu while my mother built it."

"But... I thought you built it," I said. My head was beginning to ache, but I had to continue.

"I changed it to my liking, but it was given to me by my mother, and I serve at her behest. When she came to me and asked that I keep the souls of the gods in my world, like a prison, I agreed." He turned away. "I wanted to be a good son and look what it got me."

"I'm sorry," I said, my head nearly splitting in two. "My head is killing me."

He choked back a tear. "We should stop, then. It's best. We should continue our search."

"What are we looking for again?" I whispered to him through the scorching pain in my head.

"The Jabberwocky of Antioch. A monster from my mother's collection."

I rubbed my forehead, and my headache subsided. "What does a Jabberwocky look like?"

"Beware the Jabberwock, my son!" Hypnos said, sadly. "The jaws that bite, the claws that catch! Beware the Jubjub bird and shun. The frumious Bandersnatch!"

"I remember that, vaguely." I said. "Alice in Wonderland, right?"

"It ended up contained in those pages by a muse that knew him, but my brother spoke those words first. It was all nonsense, but he liked this one monster above all others." Hypnos looked over to the bed. "There it is." He reached over and picked up a brown monster with long teeth and big, innocent eyes. I thought to myself that it looked like Domo, but then realized, if anything, Domo looked like it. "The Jabberwocky, my father. I have procured it."

The stuffed animal was worn to the nub, with barely any hair anymore. "It doesn't look like much. Why does your father want it?"

"Who knows? And why couldn't he get it himself? No idea, but now we have it, so I expect he'll tell us what he wants with it. Either that, or this was all a stupid mission to teach me some damned thing or another. He better give me the key or I'll kill him. Barring that, I'll die trying. I am sick of his games. Always his games, and my mother went along with it."

"Who was your mother?"

"Nox," Hypnos said with a sigh. "They were the literal worst—*are* the literal worst. Guess they are both alive, watching their children kill each other. That sounds like them." He gave the Jabberwocky a menacing squeeze.

I studied him for a long moment before finally saying, "You sound like there's something you really want to say, but you're not telling me."

The smile he gave me was fake. "My dear, there are hundreds of things I am not telling you. My family is complicated, like all others, but they are also gods, which means they had responsibilities, and so did we." He sighed. "I do not want your head to explode, so I will simply say that I wish it had been different." He squeezed the Jabberwocky again. "But it wasn't, and there is no way to fix it, not even for a god."

I placed my hand on his, took a deep breath of Mount Olympus air, and reveled in the weirdness of my life. "Then let's get you home. Maybe you can't fix your past, but we can still save the future of the Dream Realm."

He smiled again, but there was sincerity behind it this time. "Yes, let us."

CHAPTER 39
AINE

We descended into darkness. Clotho, holding a small lantern, led the pack of refugees—dozens of my people from Oz mixed with the Mountain People, whose glowing locks cast eerie shadows on the walls. Lachesis was in the back with another small lantern. The only other light was me, glowing a dim purple in the darkness; the last of my kind.

The cavern was cool, and it became cooler with every step. It was a refreshing change from the Spindle, which had been insufferably hot with all of the refugees huddled inside. The sound from the monsters had dimmed as we descended, but a new fear gripped me: the fear of Agrona, and what we would find in the darkness.

I fluttered closer to Clotho. "Did you bring Chelle here as well?"

"No," Clotho said. "She came on her own."

"Why did you make her walk to her death alone?"

A smile pulled at the corners of her mouth. "We had to wait for you."

"For us? So you knew we were coming?" I asked. "Did you have a vision?"

"We knew it was likely, given what we could see. We cannot see everything, and we cannot tell what will definitely happen. Only what is likely to happen."

"And...what is likely to happen now?" I asked with trepidation.

She shook her head. "If I were to tell you that, it would change the likelihood of it happening."

"Are we all going to die?" I asked slowly.

"If I told you yes, would you follow me, and do what needs to be done?" she asked, pointedly. There was no bitterness on her tongue.

I shook my head. "I don't know. Did you tell Chelle she was going to die?"

Clotho sighed. "Never in so many words, but she knew her fate."

"And she still went through with it?"

"Yes," Clotho said with a nod, slowly descending onto another uneven step. "She went to her destiny with honor and gave us a chance to save everything."

"And gave Epiales a chance to destroy everything."

"I do not know his true aim. He could create, or destroy, but given his nature, the former is not likely. I only know that he cannot be allowed to take control of the Heart. If he does, the arc of the universe will bend to tragedy."

"Why did Chelle restart it, then, if it was so dangerous for her to do so?"

"Because even with the risk, it was our best shot at stopping Epiales. If we get to the Heart first, then we will be at our most powerful. Should Hypnos come, then he will be at his most powerful in the Heart as well."

"Won't Epiales be at his most powerful as well?"

"Not as powerful as Hypnos." Clotho shook her head. "He is the thing of nightmares, while he is stronger than almost any other god in this place, his mother and Hypnos both dwarf his power here. He has no natural connection with the Heart. He must steal his connection. If he establishes one, though, his rule will be total. We must not let that happen."

"You said this all rested on Hypnos. Will he really come?"

Clotho shrugged. "There are wheels in motion that could bring him to us, but that path is hazier to us. I only know my path, and now I must walk it."

"I hope you are right."

"If we are not, then we will face that burden. It will not be the first time."

"Then why should we follow you?" I asked. "If all you do is send people to their deaths without even knowing if it's the right path?"

"We have seen through time and space, and this is our best chance for success. Everything we have done, our whole lives have led us here to this moment, to what we do now. We will not fail if there is an ounce of life left in us." Clotho looked at me. "Do you believe me?"

"I do."

"Good," she replied. "Much will be asked of you before the end. My sister does not believe you will rise to the occasion, but I do."

"If the snarky Gorgon Chelle can fulfill her destiny and die for the cause, I can handle any destiny made for me."

"We shall see," Clotho said, taking a long, deep breath. "We should conserve our energy. There is a long way to go."

Clotho did not want to speak any more, but I still had questions. I looked back at the refugees. They were my charge. I didn't care if I died, I would do all I could to protect them. I flew backwards through the people climbing down the stairs with me, trudging through the darkness on my command. They trusted me.

"Where are you going?" a woman asked. "Are you leaving?"

I shook my head. "No, I just wanted to see all of you. Everything is okay. I promise."

She smiled at me, and I could tell she believed me more than I believed myself. Nothing was okay. I took a deep sigh as I fluttered to the back of the group.

"You shouldn't lie to them," Lachesis grumbled from several steps behind me. "Nothing will be all right."

"That's not what Clotho told me. She said this was our best chance."

Lachesis scoffed. "Our best chance, maybe, but that doesn't mean it's a good chance."

I stared intently at her, studying her responses. "She seems to think it will all be okay."

"She does," Lachesis said, nodding. "She does at that. She's also an idiot."

It was hard for me not to laugh, and Lachesis smiled at me. "So do you not think we will survive?" I asked.

The Gorgon shrugged. "It depends on many, many factors. Will Hypnos get the key? Will he come to us? Will Nox part with her key? Will the Red Rider make it to us? Will we be able to fend off Epiales when he comes— because he will come. I can feel him and Agrona even now. They are nearly to the core."

"There's no way we can fight against both of them."

"No, not for long, but that doesn't mean we shouldn't try, I suppose. Worst that happens is we die, and then at least this will all be over, right?"

I nodded.

She shrugged. "And who knows, maybe we'll win. Better than sitting in that tower. I don't think I could have stomached it for one more day."

"I suppose so."

"Did Clotho tell you about your part in this?" Lachesis asked.

"She only said I had a part, but not what it was."

"I can do no better, except to say that when the moment comes, look to your past to find your way forward."

"Very cryptic. Thanks, I hate it."

She laughed. "It is the way of the Fates, but I promise when you are in the moment, you will find it to be helpful."

"And until then?"

"Until then," she said with a chuckle. "You brood."

CHAPTER 40
NIMUE

"How much further?" We were making our way to the fake Parthenon's basement. I had to admit, I was very sick of creepy, dark places. Wherever I ended up, it would be filled with light.

The torch Thanatos carried lit the smile on his face. "Not far, but do not be so hasty." His voice took on a deeper tone and echoed against the walls. "There are traps laid throughout the labyrinth, and should you make it through, a beast rests at its center so fearsome that it will rip you asunder if you make one false move."

Gwen rolled her eyes. "That's what they always say." She ran her fingers along the exposed brick and lifted a thick layer of caked dust from the wall. "When was the last time you let somebody down here?"

Thanatos scoffed. "I cannot even remember the last one who had the gall to seek the statue."

"So that's what we're after?" I asked. "I thought you said it was a key."

"I suppose I did," he replied. "The statue is what the

monster guards, but the true treasure is bound within the statue, a key to imagination so grand that—"

"We get it," Gwen said abruptly. "The key leads to the Dream Realm. You don't have to keep up with the theatrics. We're already here. You've sold us on this dungeon, and as any good salesman will tell you, once you've sold the goods, quit selling."

We reached the bottom of the stairs. "Good, because we're here." Thanatos handed the torch to me and wiped his forehead with the back of his hand. "The statue's at the center of the maze with the beast. If you make it there and back, it will be nice to see you again."

"But the odds are low," I said.

He nodded slowly. "Infinitesimal. My traps are devilishly clever. I would be surprised if you lasted even ten minutes."

"Thanks for the vote of confidence," I muttered as he walked up the stairs and out of sight. I held up the torch and looked down each side of the hallway. I noticed a soft blue light in Gwen's hand, which turned into a bright light a moment later.

"Where are we going?" Gwen said, holding her electronic tablet into the air. Its bright light drowned out my torch. "Left or right?"

"I don't know. I've never been here before."

"Don't you have the map?" Gwen asked, impatience in her voice.

"Oh yeah," I snickered. "You said it was a children's toy."

She let out an exasperated breath. "Well, that was before we knew there was a crazy labyrinth under the store, wasn't it? Now, it seems to make a whole lot more sense."

I pulled the map out of my pocket and unfolded it. The

maze was intricate, but the answer was drawn in bright orange on top of the map, belying its complexity. "I think we go right."

Gwen looked over my shoulder. "Let's just hope whoever's kid drew this knew what they were doing."

We turned up the hall, inching along to avoid any traps. Gwen shined her light on the walls, looking for them, but we didn't find any along the first wall. At the first fork, we turned left. We made it halfway down the hallway before I heard a creak under me, and then the ground gave way.

"Jump!" I shouted, hopping out of the way.

But my alarm was unnecessary. The trapped door under us slid open partially, and then jammed. I tiptoed over the gap and noticed the rusty spikes underneath. I knelt and felt the tip of one. "Dull."

"These stupid temples never keep up with their maintenance. They just expect things to keep working, like magic." Gwen tsked. "There was a time this place might have been scary, but I suspect we're going to find a lot of unmaintained traps." She nodded to herself as she continued. "Still, that could be the trap...they get us to put our guard down. I doubt it, though. The gods like to think they are tricky, but they are never as tricky as they think. They are lazier than you would believe."

Gwen wasn't wrong. We made a left and then two rights, and came upon a wall with a hundred arrows, wood rotted at the base, sticking into it. Below the wall, a skeleton, mostly rotted away, had an arrow sticking out of its eye.

"At least we know that this place was formidable once." Gwen pressed her foot against the skeleton's torso and popped its arm from its shoulder. It had been so long since I had seen a dead person that I forgot how creepy they were.

For the last several eons, I had only seen the dead as scattered bits of ash. The rattling of the bones sent a shiver up my spine.

"What are you doing with that dead thing? Show some respect," I said.

"He's dead. He's not using this body anymore," Gwen said. She tossed the arm across the length of the wall until it safely landed on the other side of the wall of arrows. "See, they never reload these things either. Come on."

Gwen grabbed an arrow and pulled herself up onto one and placed her other foot on another arrow higher on the wall. The arrows bent and creaked, but they did not break, and Gwen climbed until her head was above the wall of the labyrinth. She pulled up her phone and looked across the labyrinth. "Looks like we're close."

I looked down at my map. "Yes, a few more turns and we'll be in the center."

"That wasn't so hard," Gwen said, jumping down. "What do you think is in there?"

I shrugged. "If it's anything like the old stories, I suppose a Minotaur. Possibly a hydra. I don't know if we'll be able to defeat either without magic."

Gwen brushed dust off of her pants and shot me with a smile. "With any luck, it will be as malnourished as the rest of this place is poorly maintained."

I liked Gwen. Nothing fazed her. I was used to non-royal people being skittish and indecisive, but Gwen was confident and strong, two qualities I admired about myself.

We turned left, and at the end of that hallway came to a large circle that reminded me of a gladiatorial ring. A large, raised platform sat in the center. "That must be it."

"Be careful," Gwen said. "We don't know what to expect. You look left. I'll go right."

As I rounded the circle, Gwen screamed a curse that sent me running toward her, throwing caution to the wind. "Are you okay?"

"Yeah!" she said with a snicker. "This is just absolutely bonkers. Get over here."

When I reached her, I saw her kneeling in front of the bones of a huge bull-like monster, with a large golden ring in its skeletal nose. Like the rest of the labyrinth, it was coated with a thick layer of dust. "That's a shame."

Gwen turned to me. "I know, right? I mean, I didn't want to get eaten by her, but I didn't want her to starve to death, either. This is totally sad." She pushed up and brushed off her hands. "Oh well. That's done. Shall we see what the big fuss was all about in building this place?"

I nodded and followed her toward the pedestal in the center of the room. I expected to find a statue, but I only found a piece of paper. "Is this some kind of joke?"

She shrugged. "I don't know. This whole place is kind of a joke, so maybe."

I picked up the note and opened it. I furrowed my brow as I read. *Thank you for your contribution to the Paso Robles American History Museum.*

CHAPTER 41

RED

Ariel swam through the dark water without the benefit of a light or glowing eyes, and yet she never wavered. Even though she was not as fast a swimmer as Eyo, what with her human legs and all, she was no less confident.

"Why do you stay down here, at the bottom of the sea?"

Ariel smiled. "It's quiet down here. Nobody trying to kill you. Nobody trying to take your crown. Just the simple peacefulness of the ocean, and you drifting around in it."

"Who were you?" I asked, kicking my feet to keep up with her. Though she was not a fish, she had clearly lived under the ocean for a long time and developed strong swimming instincts. "When you were up there?"

"Do you remember the story of the drowned princess?" Her voice was dispassionate though it contained a hint of regret.

If I had access to air, I would have gasped, but instead when I opened my mouth bubbles blew out of my lips. I had indeed heard the story of the drowned princess. Three hundred years ago, there was a war in Urgu for the throne of Oz. The queen at the time had a protegee, who everyone was sure would be the next queen. Even Hypnos favored her. A group of usurpers captured the princess and threatened to kill the princess should the queen not abdicate.

When the queen acquiesced to their demands, they killed her and fed the princess to the mermaids as a cautionary tale. When Hypnos found the usurpers, he dusted them all in his grief and didn't give another blessing for a hundred years, sparking a civil war that killed twenty percent of souls in Urgu. Finally, Hypnos named Ozma to the throne, and peace reigned...until it didn't.

"That was you?"

"It was. Politics never suited me on the surface. Here... well, I have never been betrayed under the sea." Ariel stopped swimming and floated. "We are here."

My eyes had adjusted to the darkness, and I could see the outline of the cave. "What will I find inside?" I asked.

"Nox is the goddess of the night. Out of respect for her, we do not use any light to find her. Those that can come upon her using only their wits are granted an audience and can ask a favor of her."

I glanced at Ariel. "What did you ask?"

"I asked to be allowed to stay here, with her, and to make the mermaids my new people. She agreed. She can be very reasonable, in the right mood. I hope you find her in such a mood today."

I nodded and kicked my legs toward the cave, which was as black as any I had ever seen or felt. It wasn't long before Ariel was lost to my sight. I couldn't even see my hand in front of my face. The abyss washed over me, and I was overcome.

"You are who Anansi sent?" Nox said. Her voice seemed to come from every angle. "I thought I might have garnered a little more respect than one human without an ounce of royal blood in her."

"I served the Queen of Oz."

"Yes, multiple queens, if memory serves, and you watched two of them die. How was your service taken by them, in the end?"

I dropped my head to my chest. "It was a mistake that they died, but it was not my mistake to carry alone."

"Were you not charged with protecting them?"

"Not I alone," I replied. "Besides, that is hardly the point now, is it?"

"Isn't it? I know what you come to ask, and yet you have failed to protect a human, twice. What chance do you have of protecting all of Urgu from a god—from my son?"

"I do not have to protect it. You could come with me and do what must be done. Since you choose to remain here, I have to bear the burden until it kills me."

A thin laugh. "Do you even know what must be done, child?"

I shook my head. "I only know my charge, which was to find the key and return it to Sekhmet."

"But she is dead, and so is Anansi. There are few alive in Urgu that know how the key works, and yet, without it, you risk losing everything." There was silence. Nox was some-how...searching me. "You have known loss, have you not?"

"You know I do," I said, my voice hot with anger. "I'm not certain if I will succeed in my quest. I only know my charge. But as you pointed out, all those I have been loyal to are dead now. I suppose I have nothing to offer to your service except myself."

"You think I want that? You are a death sentence."

"It is what I have to offer you. My service, for the rest of my days, however long or short they may be."

"And what would I do with the charge of a human? You parlay weakly."

I reached into my pocket and pulled out the spider Anansi had given me and pulled off the amulet from Sekhmet. "These items were given to me by the gods. I offer them as well in exchange for your help. Your children are—"

"Piffle. My children are spoiled. I gave them everything, and they gave it all up. Hypnos returning to Earth and Epiales throwing a temper tantrum. I hoped they would both come to their senses and work this out, but that is unlikely."

"They could, still...if you talked some sense into them."

"I am their mother, not their counsel. There is a chance they will not come to blows, but it fades with every step Epiales takes toward the Heart."

"Then why don't you help? You are their mother. You could—"

"They are adults."

"If you don't help, this place might be destroyed. The Dream Realm, the Nightmare Realm, all of it."

"My dear, I constructed this place from scratch. I can do it again if I choose, but if I intervene, my children will learn nothing."

"Does that mean you will not help me?"

"I didn't say that, child." Out of the darkness something appeared in front of me. It gave a small glow at first, then the light spread. "In the room where they keep the Heart of Urgu there is a hidden door. That door has a keyhole, a tiny hole notched in the wall. This key will open it, and if the door on the other side is opened at the same time, Hypnos will be able to return."

"Will he come to us?"

"He is trying," she said. "But if Hypnos can come in, so Epiales can escape, and if Epiales escapes, he will wreak havoc on the universe. You must not let that happen."

"How can I stop him?"

"I don't know. So, my charge, this is my first quest for you."

"I accept." I had been in the service of powerful beings my whole life, and now was no different. "How do I get to the Heart?"

"I will show you," Nox said. "And if you are successful, my child, you must ask Hypnos a favor."

"What is it?"

"To return you to Earth. I have no use for you here, but I have need of eyes back on Earth for what is to come."

"That's impossible. How can you—"

"Nothing is impossible. Nimue accomplished it, though her return was conducted hastily and sloppily. A god can do it much easier, given the right motivation."

"What is to com—"

"He will know what to do," Nox said, unable or unwilling to answer my question. "Do you understand?"

I grabbed the key. "I do."

A thin light appeared in the distance and Nox spoke one last time. "Follow the light, and you will find the Heart."

CHAPTER 42

AINE

A pinprick of light became a welcome flood of brightness when we reached the bottom of the stairs and stood before a cavern. I had no idea how long we descended into the depths of Urgu. I flew up to Clotho.

"Is this it?" I asked.

"Nearly," she replied, taking a step inside the cave. "But we are not there yet."

She turned down a thin path. The massive cavern was so enormous I could barely make out the other side. Along the walls pink dream orbs glittered, and when I fluttered above, I could see pink from the orbs pulsating at the bottom of the fissure.

"This place used to be filled with dreams," Clotho said. "As high as the cave itself. When we stopped the Heart, no new dreams came for a century. Now, it begins to fill again." She faltered. "Brings a tear to this old Gorgon's eye. One day, if we can stay alive long enough, it will be filled again."

We neared a pale blue light against the pink, creating a pastel glow like my own skin. It was a pixie, sitting against the side of the cavern, looking over the edge and kicking his legs from one side to the other.

"Aimon!" Clothos said. "What ho, old friend?"

Aimon turned, half-heartedly, to see hundreds of us walking toward him, and his eyes went wide. "Back! Back! Back! You are not welcome in the Heart of Urgu."

I had heard stories of the great pixie warrior Aimon, plucked from service to the queen and endowed by Hypnos with the power to protect the Heart for as long as it beat, and clearly even longer.

Clotho held up her hands. "It's okay, Aimon. Do you remember me? When I was young to this world, we were acquainted."

Aimon narrowed his eyes. "The Fate, yes? Which are you?"

"Clotho," she said, pointing behind her. "Back there, she is Lachesis. And I fear you know what happened to the third."

Aimon looked down. "She was brave to the end. And she succeeded. Do you see that the cavern fills again with millions of dreams? Soon...soon...it will rise into the heavens again, just like the days of old."

Clotho smiled. "I do see, my friend, but that is why we are here. I'm afraid dark times have come from Urgu above. Do you feel them?"

He nodded, peering upwards. "I feel the darkness coming. Even now the gods break our defenses to get to the Heart. I worry they will succeed where they failed so many times before."

"They will," I said with fear in my throat. He might be the last fairy, besides me, and I wanted him to be safe with us. However, I feared he had a job to do.

"If they come, then you must be ready," Clotho said.

"Buying us time will be of the essence. Every moment counts."

"Yes, my fate, but...you must know I cannot hold them off for long. I am the most powerful fairy that ever existed, and Hypnos endowed me with great gifts on top of that, but I cannot beat a god, not on my own."

"This is true," Clotho said. "You might die."

"I have waited my whole life to choose to die for what I believe in. It would be a great honor to die for you."

"No, you must live!" I dropped my eyes. "You might be the last of us in this place, aside from me. We two have a legacy, and we must rise to the occasion."

He took a somber tone. "Yes, your majesty."

"Come," Clotho said, moving past the fairy. She ran her fingers against the rock wall. "There is much to do."

"Perhaps I should help him," I said, landing on Clotho's shoulder.

Clotho shook her head. "No, I need you with me. I have foreseen it."

"You can get somebody to do just about anything if you say 'I have foreseen it,' you know?"

"That's not true. If it were, we would not be in this place, and Epiales would be satiated to return to his realm."

I chose not to respond, though I was still pretty certain I was correct. Instead, I just watched Clotho close her eyes as she walked along the wall, stopping at a hundred paces from me. She mumbled something under her breath and a door revealed itself. The same assortment of metallic snakes that adorned the door in the Spindle rested in the middle of this one, waiting for Clotho's touch.

Her hand began to glow, and she placed it at the center of the snakes. Their eyes glowed red as they made a familiar pattern, locked in place, and the door opened.

"This way," Clotho said, disappearing behind the door.

I flew forward into a long hallway and I was awash in a vibrant pink glow. Dream orbs lined the corridors, whose walls danced with beauty and majesty. There were dreams of every type, from playful to adventurous, from simple to complex. It filled my heart with joy.

At the end of the hallway, the walls broke into a circular room. At its center sat an enormous orb, a hundred times bigger and more vibrantly pink than any of the others. Instead of dreams dancing inside, this orb was filled with the outlines of sleeping people, thousands of them swirled around and danced around each other inside of it.

Clotho smiled. "I forgot how beautiful it was." She took a deep sigh and turned to me. "Gather the refugees behind the Heart. We will make our stand here."

CHAPTER 43
NIMUE

"What is this about?" I screamed at Thanatos as we stomped back into the store. It took us almost no time to exit the maze, and the fire in my belly hastened our exit.

"My," Thanatos said. "You were quick. Did the Minotaur give you no trouble?"

"She was dead," Gwen said, deadpan.

"Oh my," he said, hand on his chest. "That couldn't be."

"And there was no statue...or anything," I added.

"That's impossible. I have kep—"

"No, it's not," I butted in, handing him the note. "All I found was this note."

Thanatos read the note and sighed. "This is not good."

I put my hands on my hips. "I thought you said nobody had come here in years."

"Ah yes, I understand." Thanatos scratched his head. "There was a break-in several months ago, but I thought it was just some silly teenagers."

"And you didn't bother to check out the basement?"

He shrugged. "Labyrinths take care of themselves."

"No, dude," Gwen said. "They don't. That place is a death trap, and not in the way you intended. It looked like it hadn't been maintenanced in a hundred years. There's rusty spikes and loose arrows everywhere."

"That is very troubling." Thanatos moved behind his counter, tapping the glass next to his register. "I see you have my map. I would appreciate it back."

"I—" I started before Gwen cut in front of me.

"How important is it to you?" she asked with a smile.

Thanatos shrugged. "It reminds me of my child, who solved it when he was a wee tot. I do not have many memories of him, so it is quite precious to me."

"Then how about a trade?" she said.

"How about I kill you and take it?" Thanatos said flatly. "That is my vocation after all."

"I mean, you could, but then you'd have a mess, and I'm not going to ask for much."

Thanatos sighed. "What do you ask then?

"Do you have a picture of this statue so we can go looking for it?" Gwen asked.

"I think so." Thanatos rummaged under his desk for a moment and then pulled up a picture. "Ah, here it is."

"Can we have it?" Gwen held up the map. "Fair trade. In fact, I think you're getting the better end of the deal."

Thanatos grumbled. "Fine, as long as it gets me out of this annoying conversation."

"It does." Gwen snatched the picture from Thanatos's hand and gave him the map. "Come on, Nimue. We have more work to do."

I looked from Thanatos to Gwen, the map to the picture in her hand, my mouth open. "This is stupid."

"Welcome to questing."

It took us until the following morning to arrive at Paso Robles. Gwen told me that we could go wine tasting once this was over, which sounded lovely. I needed to wash the bitter taste of this adventure out of my mouth.

I spent most of the drive looking at the photograph of the statue. I couldn't get over how...unimpressive it was in every respect. The statue, chipped and cracked over the centuries, was that of a portly woman with sagging breasts. Her face was worn and the detail in the clothing had been eroded by time. Anything I saw in Thanatos's store was more impressive than the squat woman we were traveling to find.

The Paso Robles American History Museum was tucked off from the main road, away from residences, up on a hill that overlooked the city. The view from the top of the hill stretched for miles, and I could see thousands of homes.

Glass doors slid open to greet us. A cold blast of air met me as I stepped through into the lobby. On either side of us, glass cabinets showcased pots and bowls, equally banal and unimpressive as the statue for which we searched.

"Why would somebody come to this museum to see a bowl?" I asked, peering down to get a closer look.

"People love looking at old stuff. Like, absolutely love it."

"I don't get it. I grew up in the time when many of these were made and they would have been unremarkable then. What makes them remarkable now?"

Gwen shrugged. "They lasted, I suppose. Just surviving a long time is impressive in its own right."

"Fair enough," I replied, standing upright. "Do you know what we're looking for?"

Gwen nodded. "Yup. A squat, portly statue of a woman

that looks like it's gone through the wash about a million times. You take one side, and I'll take the other. We'll meet in the middle, okay?"

I nodded. "Sounds good."

I broke away from Gwen and started walking through the museum. If it was any indication of America, then America was both quite full of itself and exceedingly boring. I looked down at the picture to get another sense of the statue. It was, just like the rest of the museum, quite dull and unremarkable, except for its age. However, if age was the only requirement, I suppose I should have been an exhibit myself, and I would have made a better exhibit than a stupid bowl.

I looked all around the museum but finished my search uninspired and without any idea where the statue might be. An hour after we started, I met Gwen in the middle of the museum, completely fruitless.

"Find anything?" I asked.

"Nothing," Gwen replied. "Guess you didn't find anything, either."

"Nope." I shook my head. "Absolutely zilch."

"Let's go find somebody who can help us." She ripped the picture from my hand and stormed up to the front desk. "Excuse me?"

A bald man with glasses looked up at us. "Can I help you?"

"Have you seen this around here?" She held up the picture of the statue to the man.

"We're kind of looking for it."

The man took a look and scoffed. "That old thing. Somebody came in and told me it was from the 1700s. Can you believe the gall on them?"

"So...it wasn't?"

"It was a cheap fake and completely unremarkable. I gave him $50 and put it in our woman's room. Waste of money and time. I feel bad for the old chap. He's usually not easily fooled."

"So..." Gwen said. "If we gave you $100 could we have it?"

"You know what?" the man said. "It offends my taste to take money for it. It would be an honor to have you take it off my hands."

"Really?" Gwen said. "Just like that?"

"Absolutely," he said, turning back to his computer. "Get it out of my museum before somebody realizes what an abomination it is."

I followed Gwen into the bathroom. We squeezed inside, and there, on the top of the toilet on a small shelf, nestled between scentless flowers, the fat, old lady statue smiled at us.

I picked up the statue. "Too bad he has no idea what he's got here."

"Well, not really. It's better he doesn't know, so we don't have to steal it."

"What do we do now?"

"I guess...break it?"

I shrugged, lifted the statue over my head, and dropped it on the checkered tile. It felt good to break something, and not be the thing being broken. Gwen brushed through the debris before popping up with a long, golden key, gnarled at the end, and nearly as long as her palm.

"What's going on in there?" the man's voice said from the other side of the door.

I cracked the door and smiled at him. "Nothing. I'm sorry, but I think we broke your worthless statue." I pulled

Gwen out of the bathroom as the man stood, shaking his head at the mess on the floor. "Have a great day."

Come now. Etsop's voice boomed through my head. His voice was so powerful that I thought my head would explode. *Don't dawdle, and tell Rose and Hypnos to meet you here.*

ROSE

Bang. Bang. Bang.

Hypnos's fist slammed against the door to his father's house. "Open up!"

He squeezed the Jabberwocky stuffed animal in his hand. If it were a real live monster, he would have choked it to death by now. Another round of banging, and I heard movement on the other side of the door. A moment later, Erebus opened the door and stood leaning against the door jamb.

"You're going to cause a scene, Junior," he said, his eyes swirling like the universe lived inside his pupils.

Hypnos held up the Jabberwocky. "I brought it."

Erebus smiled. "Do you remember what Epiales used to say? The tide that binds. The teeth that move. Stop the Jabberwock, my dad."

"That's not what he said," Hypnos grumbled. "Take it."

Erebus shook his head. "I don't want it."

"I don't care." Hypnos gritted my teeth. "Take it or don't but give me the key."

"I don't have it."

Hypnos balled his fists. "Then what was this all for?"

"A reminder," Erebus said. "Your brother wasn't always a monster. For a time, he was a kid, wild and free. He was a gentle soul. Do you remember that? He saved birds and protected trees. He didn't even like stepping on ants."

"I remember," Hypnos said. He dropped the Jabberwock to his side and gave it a wistful smile. "He would bring them to the edge of Mount Olympus and wave as they crawled away. But he's not that person anymore. Now, he's a monster."

Erebus shook his head. "No, he's still not a monster. He's just misguided, vengeful, and bitter. I'm afraid I am partially to blame for that."

"Partially? You and Mom were horrible. The worst. It's shocking that I ended up as well adjusted as I did."

"You didn't," Erebus said, flatly. "Nobody grows up well adjusted. We just keep giving different complexes to our children. We compensate for one insecurity and give our offspring two more."

"And what is my insecurity, Dad?"

"That's easy," Erebus said smoothly. "You're a mama's boy. She loved you most, and you let her hide from the universe for too long. Meanwhile, your brother has been in the dark and cold all his life. Epiales is jealous of you. That's why he's lashing out."

"And threatening to kill millions of my people."

"Not just your people. Once he's done with the Dream Realm, he'll set off across the universe until he's had his fill of bloodlust." Erebus sighed. "Anything to get your mother's attention. That's why I sent you to fetch the Jabberwocky. You are both our children, and we love you, but you are still children. When you face your brother, remember that."

"And how will I face him, without the key?"

"They already have it," Erebus said. "Your friends recovered it for you, and now wait at the demon's pet shop for you to meet them." He turned to me. "They tried to call you, but your phone is still lost."

"Thank you," I said.

"Don't thank him," Hypnos grumbled. "This is all his fault."

Erebus started to close the door. "You would blame me. Perhaps one day you will see the truth."

"Not likely," Hypnos said. The door clicked closed. "Let's just get away from here."

I grabbed Hypnos's hand and together we vanished. When we reappeared, we were standing in the entrance of Etsop's pet shop.

"That's not fair!" Nimue said. "I've done everything you asked."

As we walked to the back of the store, we came upon Nimue, Gwen, and Etsop standing in a circle. Nimue was shaking her hands angrily at the demon, who leaned back on his heels, barely registering her indignation.

"You sound like a child," he said. "I won't let you out of your contract. Not when you've proven to be so valuable." Etsop looked at me. "Oh, good, you've arrived."

"What's she doing here?" I said, throwing Nimue a dark look.

Gwen stepped forward, poking her finger in my chest. "She's the one who found your stupid key, so show her some respect."

"That would imply I should listen to a word you said, traitor," I sneered. "And that I had an ounce of respect for her in the first place."

"Ladies, gentlemen, gods," Etsop said. "I am happy to

say that Miss Gwen is 100 percent truthful in her statement." He held up the key in his hand. "And I happen to have that which you seek."

"How did you find it?" Hypnos asked.

Etsop stuck out his concave chest proudly. "Once I knew what you were after, it was a simple matter to track it down with the help of my lovely assistants. I will give it to you. My price is a simple favor from a god."

"I am not your assistant, dude," Gwen said. "And please never call me lovely again."

"So touchy," Etsop said. "What do you say, Hypnos? Is it a deal?"

"You'll never get me in your debt," Hypnos said, looking over at Nimue. "I've seen what you do to those who owe you."

"Very well." Etsop shrugged. "I'm sure there are others who would pay for such a powerful artifact."

He turned away, but I moved forward to stop him. "Wait." I pulled the necklace off my body. "I have an amulet that allows the wearer to enter Mount Olympus. That has to be more valuable than some stupid key to the Dream Realm, especially if Epiales destroys it all."

Etsop thought for a moment. "The power of a god, and you give it up. You must really want to save your girlfriend."

"I do."

"Very well, you have a deal."

I grabbed the key from him and handed him the necklace. "Thank you."

"And what about me?" Gwen said. "I was promised that Hypnos would help my boyfriend if I helped you."

"You left!" I shrieked. "You went off with a butcher and a monster!"

"Be that as it may," Gwen said. "I still helped. A lot."

"Yes, you did. I will keep my word." Hypnos looked around at the shelves. "Do you happen to have a vial, Etsop?"

"Of course," Etsop said with a nod, turning to his counter. "I'll even give you one on the house, proving I am a kind, merciful and helpful demon."

Etsop curled his bony fingers, searching around under the table until he pulled up a glass vial. He handed it to Hypnos, who removed the rubber stopper and placed the open vial against his face. Three tears dropped from his eye, collected in the small container. They glowed pink and looked as if they were swirled with glitter.

"Here," Hypnos said as he capped the vial and handed it to Gwen. "Have him drink this, and he will see clearly again."

"That's it? Just this little bit?" Gwen asked.

"It is all that is needed."

Gwen nodded. "Thank you."

"Good for you. All of you," Nimue grumbled. "So everyone gets what they want except for me? Brilliant."

"You wanted to come to Earth," Etsop said, "And that has a price."

"I suppose you deserve help, too." Hypnos sighed and held up the Jabberwocky. "This is from Mount Olympus, the personal collection of Epiales himself. I offer it as a trade for Nimue's life."

"It is exquisite, with a special kind of power." Etsop touched the Jabberwocky. "That won't buy her freedom, though. What do you think—"

"It was Epiales's favorite, and contains bits of his hair, and the essence of godlike joy, which can be very powerful in the right hands."

Etsop thought for a moment. "It will buy her a long

vacation, but she is still in my employ, should I need her services."

"That's up to Nimue," Hypnos said.

Nimue nodded. "It's something, but stay out of my head. If you need me, call me."

"If you wish," Etsop said, taking the Jabberwocky from Hypnos's hand. "Are we all square then?"

"Square," said Gwen. "Nimue, are you coming?"

Nimue cocked her head. "You still want me to come with you, even after all the trouble I caused?"

Gwen nodded. "You're good company, and that's not an easy thing to find."

"Then I would be honored to see an end to your quest...together."

When Gwen and Nimue had left the shop. I turned to Hypnos. "You shouldn't have done that. Nimue is bad news."

"There are plenty of things worse than a witch without her powers. Don't you watch the news? Out here, she is one of the things I worry about least." He stared out the door Nimue had just exited before turning to me. "Now, I believe we have a date with a Spindle."

"Good luck," Etsop said, though his words sounded insincere.

"I don't know what game you are playing, Etsop," Hypnos said. "But whatever it is, don't get in my way."

"I wouldn't dream of it."

Hypnos grabbed my arm. I didn't like the way Etsop said those final words, either. A shiver ran over my spine as we vanished into the ether.

CHAPTER 45

AINE

"Barricade the door!" I shouted to Balor, who was nearest the door to the Heart of Urgu.

"With what?" he shouted back.

"Anything," I replied. "Epiales and Agrona aren't going to let a door stop them."

"There's nothing in here but bodies!" Balor replied, disgusted. "And the rutting Heart, that is."

It was little use, I knew. Even all the best fighters among the Mountain People could not hope to contain Epiales for more than a minute. In fact, their best fighter, Boudica, had already tried. So had Red, the single best fighter I'd ever met. She saved me, but she couldn't have survived his onslaught, not if Epiales and his monsters still came for us.

"Use your bodies! The biggest and fattest of you up front!"

I was mostly just blowing off steam, yelling to make it look like I was doing something. It was all an act. When you lead people, it was very important they saw you as in charge and actively trying to protect them. Improvisation wasn't something people praised in their leaders, but it was as important as any other skill I had developed over my long life. People needed the illusion of leadership.

Once I'd called out a few more orders, I looked around for something else I could do. Clotho and Lachesis sat on either side of me, pressing their hands against the Heart of Urgu.

"How about you?" I asked. "Any guidance?"

"Nothing we didn't already know, but the way forward clears for us," Clotho said.

"In other words, hold your horses," Lachesis added. "We're getting there."

I looked around the room. The huddled faces of fear illuminated by the pink of the Heart, and the dream orbs around the room, stared back at me, following my every movement. Across the room, the Mountain People hid their fear by standing guard behind Balor, ready for battle, as he formed the front line of our defense.

"They will come hard and fast," I said. "Gods are not known for being subtle."

"We aren't going to last long," Balor said. "I hope you have a better plan than using us for fodder."

I didn't, but I couldn't say that, so I just bit my lip. "Working on it."

Bang. Bang. Bang. The door to the Heart of Urgu shook and rattled. It was hard to swallow for the lump in my throat, and my hands were shaking. I pressed them against my body to avoid looking frightened in front of my people.

"Ready yourself!" I screamed.

"NO!" Lachesis said, opening her eyes wide. "Open the door."

"Are you crazy?" I shouted. "We're not—"

"Open the door!" Clotho chimed in, an echo of her sister. "Do it now."

"Are you sure?" I asked, whipping around to face them.

Clotho nodded. "Yes. Do it, or I will."

I sighed, staring at the floor as I spoke. "You heard her, Balor. Open the door."

"Are you crazy?" Balor shouted. "We're jammed in here!"

"Yes." I stamped my foot. "But this is all crazy, so just do it!"

Balor grumbled something under his breath, no doubt of the opinion that I was sending him to his death. He was a good soldier, though, even if a bit surly. He pushed everybody back from the door and when he unlatched it, a faint blue light fell through—Aimon. Behind the fairy stumbled another familiar face; Red, the rider, and while she was sopping wet, she looked no worse for wear.

"Gabrielle!" Balor screamed, wrapping her up in a hug. "I never thought I would see your face again."

"It's good to see you, too," she said. "Do you have a healer? This fae is injured." Balor picked Aimon up in his strong hands and brought them to the Fates.

"He was breathing shallow when I found him in the cavern," Red said. "He looked like he'd been in a great battle."

"I'm sorry," Aimon said with a whisper. "I tried—I was falling back—they are coming." He coughed feebly. "I couldn't—"

"It's okay," I said. "It's okay."

"May I die now?" he said. "Please. It is all I ever wanted, the grace of a warrior's death."

Tears filled my eyes as I nodded my head and watched him smile, his skin changing to dust. All that was left of my kind was me. I had to carry on the line of the Unseelie.

After the last of Aimon dissolved into ash, Balor spoke, turning to Red. "How did you get here?"

Red smiled. I wasn't sure I had ever seen her smile before. "It's unimportant. What matters is that I have great tidings from Nox."

Lachesis smiled. "You have the key."

Red nodded. "I do."

"Then there is still a chance."

The door shook a second time, this time harder than the last.

"Epiales is here," Clotho said, but she didn't need to. We all already knew, and the air went out of the room as we realized the end was near.

CHAPTER 46

ROSE

We appeared with a thunderous crash on the edge of a cliff. I flattened myself against the rocks to avoid plummeting hundreds of feet to my death. As I shuffled for better footing, a small pebble dislodged and barreled down hundreds of feet.

"Oh my god!" I shouted. "Where are we? It's freezing!"

Hypnos looked back at me. "You wanted to get back to the Dream Realm. I never said it would be comfortable." He walked along the cliff's edge. "It's easier to move if you lay on your stomach or crawl on all fours."

I didn't argue. I got on my knees and gripped the cliff tightly with my hands and crawled slowly behind Hypnos. I felt like an idiot, but I also felt safer on the ground when a hefty gust of wind blew, and I didn't topple over. When the path finally widened, my legs and shoulders were sore. I pushed myself to stand and looked into the mist. There was a structure there my brain seemed to recognize.

"Is that...the Spindle?" I asked, confused. It was not the regal and majestic place I remembered from the Dream Realm. This Spindle was old and decrepit. Its walls were crumbling, and it seemed to sway with each gust of wind, ready to topple at any moment.

"I don't understand. It should stand forever," Hypnos said. "I do not know why it is in such disrepair. Let's hope this works."

"Let's hope!" I shot him a look. "It better work after all of this effort."

"If it doesn't work now, the Dream Realm is doomed. I certainly hope that this wasn't for nothing."

We trudged forward through the mist. As we neared the Obsidian Spindle, the damage became even more apparent. Rocks piled at its base as if a rockslide had destroyed some of it. The exterior was still intact, but only just. Black bricks, cracked almost to a powder, were scattered in the dirt around the structure.

"Why put a Spindle all the way up here?"

"Well, we wanted it in a place that only gods could access easily. We don't need a bunch of people learning how to jump between worlds."

"Jump...between worlds? What are you talking about?"

Hypnos turned to me. "The Obsidian Spindle doesn't just take you to the Dream Realm. There is at least one on every habitable world in the galaxy. Space is difficult to manage and lonely. It's much easier to have a beacon that allows for us to travel easily between worlds."

"So there are other entrances to the Dream Realm, off of this world?"

"That's right, and other realms."

"Other...realms?"

"We really don't have time for twenty questions."

"Fair enough," I said, rubbing my temples. "This is making my brain break all over again anyway."

"Yes, it's quite a lot to grapple with. Are you sure you want to know?"

I nodded. "Absolutely."

"Fine, then. Nox built the Dream Realm, but there are all sorts of realms around the galaxy, even other sleep-based realms built by other deities. They are places where humans don't tread, but reptile people or other—anyway. That's not important." He cleared his throat and glanced at me. "There are also underworlds out there, and heavens, and all sorts of places that human beings could barely imagine. The Obsidian Spindle is how we can communicate between them and between other worlds. Urgu is but a small piece of a large, intricately-woven tapestry."

My mind was about to burst open, and if Hypnos uttered one more word it might have. Luckily, he just smiled and turned back to the Spindle. "Now, help me find the door. It's difficult to locate, especially in all this rubble."

I placed my hands on the Spindle. The brick was worn and flaked off. The roughness of the surface stung my fingers, but I would not stop. I was so close to seeing Chelle again. She and I would finally be together, and all I had to do was find one stupid door—

My left pinkie caught on a small hole and I pulled myself around to look at it. It was a divot perfect for a key. "I think I found it!"

Hypnos examined the hold. "Yes, that could certainly be it." He blew the dust from the rock aside and inserted the key. "Get ready."

The Spindle began to rotate slowly. As it did, a door appeared, made out of white light. I turned away to stop the brightness from stinging my eyes. Hypnos put on his sunglasses and turned to me.

"Let's hope the other door is open. Otherwise, this will be a very short trip."

He grabbed my hand and we walked into the light together, hoping the next stop would be the Dream Realm, and my love.

CHAPTER 47
NIMUE

Gwen drove through the night like a shrieking demon until we finally reached a small hospital on the border between California and Nevada. Oak Glen Mental Hospital.

Gwen stomped through the front door and up to a kindly man behind the counter with pink pajamas on. "I need to see Bradley Franklin." She was out of breath.

The man behind the desk looked down at his clipboard, flipping between sheets of paper. "And you are?" he asked in a calm voice.

"His girlfriend."

He didn't look up. "Gwen Palmer?"

"That's right."

"You're already on his approved contacts list." The man shook his head. "It's been a while, though, hasn't it?"

"Yeah, well...It's not the most pleasant thing to see the love of your life suffering, in pain, and unable to recognize you." She bit her lip. "But I'm here now."

He smiled. "I'm sure he'll be happy to see you."

"How is he doing?" she asked.

His eyes dropped. "It's day by day. Today is a good day. He might even talk today."

It was hard not to laugh at the irony. If Gwen was right, and Hypnos's cure worked, then he would do much more than talk today. He would be cured of whatever had destroyed his mind and able to live a life with her again.

Gwen turned back to me. "It's really happening. I can't believe it."

I grabbed her arms. "Don't get too excited. It might not—"

She pulled away from me. "It's going to work. I can feel it. I can feel it. It's got to work."

I smiled. "I hope it does. I'll be waiting right here for you—"

"No way," she said, shaking her head. "You're coming with me. This wouldn't have been possible without you and I need a friend there for moral support."

I smiled. A friend. The last time I had a friend...I killed her. This one, this one I could save, and I was excited to have the chance. "Okay. I'll come."

"Gwen," the man said. "Right this way."

Gwen grabbed my hand and squeezed it before hurrying down the hall behind the orderly. They led us into a waiting room with dozens of sad, long tables. Several other people were seated, talking to people across from them, laughing and crying in equal measure.

"Wait right here," the man said, gesturing to an empty table. When we sat down, he walked out.

"This is very sad," I said, looking around. "Is it always so sad?"

Gwen nodded. "That's why I don't do it much. There's very little hope that any of these people will ever be able to get out of here and lead a normal life. Hell, they'll barely be able to lead an abnormal one inside here."

A couple minutes of anxiety-riddled anticipation passed before the door opened again and a pasty boy with shaggy brown hair hobbled inside. His eyes were glassy with dark bags under them. They seemed to look past us as the orderly sat him down across from us. He looked as though he hadn't eaten in days and smelled like he hadn't bathed in weeks.

"Hi, Brad," Gwen said, softly. "I've missed you."

Brad didn't do anything or say anything after he sat down. He just stared off into space. Gwen reached out and grabbed his hands.

"I've done it, babe. I've done it." She reached into her pocket and pulled out the vial of Hypnos's tears. "You're not going to like this next part right now, but I swear you'll like it later."

Gwen stood up and looked at me. "Hold him still."

"What?"

Gwen spun around to the table behind Brad. "He doesn't eat or drink much. They usually have to force feed him, and they'll never let me give him a foreign substance, so please, hold him down so I can get this into him."

"Is that...legal?" I asked.

"Does it matter? What are they going to do, arrest me for curing him?" Gwen said. "Please."

I realized then that Gwen didn't actually need me for moral support. She needed me to help restrain her boyfriend. I wanted to be angry, but I had pulled enough extensive manipulation on people in my day that I could deal with a little deception against me. I stood up and walked around the table.

"Grab his hands," she said.

I did, and almost instantly he started to jerk back and fight against me. "This is for your own good."

He grunted and shook as Gwen tilted his head back and closed his nostrils together. "I'm sorry."

A group of orderlies rushed inside the room. "What are you doing?"

As they rushed her, Brad opened his mouth to breath and Gwen poured the contents of the vial in. He coughed as he swallowed the mixture at the same moment she and I were tackled.

"What were you thinking?" an older woman hissed. "You could have—"

"G-g-g-g-g-wen?" I heard softly. It was Brad. "What are you doing on the ground?"

Gwen smiled, pushing herself up from the ground, and away from one of the fatter men who had tackled her, but now was too gob smacked by what he saw to keep her contained. "Brad. You're back."

"Where am I?" he said.

"Oh, Brad." Tears filled her eyes. She wrapped her arms around him. "It's good to have you back."

I extricated myself from the grasp of the older woman holding me back and she didn't mind. We were both smiling. It was a happy ending for once, and now that Gwen had hers, it was time to make my own.

CHAPTER 48

RED

"What are you doing?" Aine asked as I walked toward the back wall of the Heart of Urgu. Her purple light combined with the pink of the walls to make a haunting, rich color. The door to the room shook violently. I could not be distracted by any more questions.

"They will be through the door in mere moments," Clotho said.

I stepped through the throngs of Dreamers to reach the far wall and ran my fingers along it, looking for a keyhole. The wall was completely smooth. It wasn't until I held the key up to the wall that a small divot appeared in the rock. I placed the key inside and turned it just as an explosion rocked the whole room.

There was nothing but dust and dirt where the front door used to be. "Balor!"

I rushed forward, leaping over the group of refugees. Little bits of ash rose into the air and the soot combined with the dirt, swirling together in a cloudy haze. Under the debris, I heard a cough, and began to dig. "Balor!"

"Get away from the door, love," Lachesis said. "Nothing bu—"

"Shut up, you old hag!" I screamed, pushing away a large rock. I saw the dirtied face of my friend and reached for his hand. I pulled as hard as I could while he pushed up from the rock pile.

"Thanks, love," he said, and I smiled at him, squeezing his shoulder. Both of us coughed a few times. "Now, if you'll excuse me."

Balor pushed away and grew into a one-eyed Cyclops, orange and snarling. Clotho and Lachesis stood, each with a glowing pink hand on the Heart. Aine's purple aura shone brighter than anything, until a white glow spilled out from the back of the room.

"The door—" I shouted.

"Hello, brother," a snarling voice said. Epiales stepped through the entryway, not a bit of soot on him. Agrona's white eyes sparkled behind him.

"Hello, Epiales," a man grunted behind me. I spun around to see a scruffy man with a long white beard and sunglasses. He took them off and his eyes glowed pink. I knew him from his visage. He was Hypnos. Next to him stood Rose, ready to fight.

CHAPTER 49

ROSE

The moment I stepped into the Dream Realm, Hypnos's power coursed through my veins. I felt like myself for the first time in a long time. I felt more powerful than myself, actually.

"Don't forget, now that you have a body, you're even more formidable," Hypnos said. "And I'm hoping we can use that to our advantage against Agrona and Epiales."

I squeezed my fists together. I hadn't used magic in several months, but I couldn't wait to do it again. I blinked and floated in the air with Hypnos, soaring above the awed men and women huddled on the floor. We landed in front of a massive pile of debris from the door collapsing upon itself. Red sat with Balor and Aine was across from them, glowing purple. Two old Gorgons stared at me, their hands glowing pink. There was no sign of Chelle.

"Hello, brother," I heard a low voice grumble. A thin, bearded man stepped through the rubble. A woman with white, glowing eyes wearing a thick coat of pelts towered over the man, even from several feet behind him.

"Epiales," Hypnos said. "You have made a mistake coming here."

"No," Epiales said. "It is you who made a mistake coming back. Now, we will end this."

"I should have killed you eons ago when I had the chance."

"You never will have the chance again." Epiales clapped his hands, and a thick stream of black ooze shot from his hands and snapped at Hypnos like a snake. Hypnos slammed his forearms together and a pink shield formed around him.

"We cannot let Epiales corrupt the Heart or hurt the souls behind us," Hypnos said, his voice echoing through the chamber. "This is our last stand."

"Right," I said. "Fireball!"

I wasn't as powerful with English spells as was with Latin, but I didn't have time to remember the old spells I had once practiced. Still, the fireball shot out of me with ferocity I had never felt before and crashed into the slate rock above Epiales.

Red crawled away from the rock as it collapsed upon the other gods. "Get back!"

Hypnos braced himself for an attack. The rock rose from the ground, covered in a green film, and shot forward at the Heart.

"Shie—"

I started to speak, but by the time the words came the two old Gorgons had thrown a protective shield over the Heart, deflecting the debris.

"We have this," one of them said. "You and Aine take care of Agrona, if you can."

I looked over at Aine, who nodded at me. We'd had an

alliance before, and now we fought together again. "How do we stop her?" I asked.

"I don't know," Aine said, fear in her eyes. "I watched her kill a god with little more than a look."

"They don't have bodies. I do. That will give me the edge."

"I can use the magic of my people," Aine said. "But I will need more power to do so and hope to control it. It is notoriously fickle."

"Give me your hand," I replied. "I have power to share."

CHAPTER 50

AINE

A surge of power rushed through me at Rose's touch. It was as if she had given me a jolt of magical energy, more than I had ever felt in my life.

"Thank you," I said.

"Don't thank me," Rose replied. "Use it."

Most magic that I cast was human magic, since I almost exclusively fought humans, but my parents had taught me the old tongue, and the powerful spells that we kept hidden from outsiders. Fairy magic was notoriously mercurial and thus I didn't like to use it unless absolutely necessary.

"*Tyll y gallon!*" I shouted, and a long spindle of pink fire shot forward toward Agrona. She tried to block it, but the light shot right through her. She collapsed for a moment, then rose.

"Even your magic could not pierce my heart, fairy," Agrona said.

"Wind blast!" Rose shouted, and she shot Agrona into the air, crashing into the wall.

"Do you have anything stronger?"

I looked back over at Clotho, who nodded. This was

why I had been brought here, my purpose. Epiales knew that there was a fairy spell that could kill a god, and it was the only thing that could protect him from Hypnos. As I stared at the old Gorgon, my mother's teachings flowed through me, and I remembered the spell.

I turned to Rose. "There is a spell that can kill Epiales, but I am not powerful enough to cast it."

"Maybe I can," she said.

"It is very dangerous," I replied. "If you utter it even one syllable wrong, you will only kill yourself. You are not fae. There is no chance for you to speak our language correctly without at least a decade of practice."

"Then you do it, but we're running out of options here!"

"In order to speak it, blood must course through my veins."

Rose, without hesitation, held out her arm to me. "Take the power you need from me."

"That is not—"

"Just do it!"

Would it work? Could it work? Fairies in the old land were known to feed on human blood, but I had not needed it while I was in the Dream Realm. Anything was worth trying. I opened my mouth and pierced Rose's skin at the wrist. She winced as I drained her blood.

The warm blood coated my throat and I trembled with delight. It pulsated through me. I felt alive for the first time in an eon. I could have nursed on her forever, but I came to my senses and unlatched from her wrist.

"That's enough," I replied.

"I am coming for you, mortal," Agrona said with a snarl. Balor, transformed into his Cyclops form, smashed forward and punched her in the face. She barely winced, and with a single blow, slammed Balor into the rock across the room before turning to Rose again. "Now you."

"No!" I flew to block Rose from harm. *"Die lle rydych chi'n sefyll!"*

A lightning bolt made of red fire shot through the air and crashed into Agrona. She took a step forward, but as she did, her leg began to fade away.

"What is happening?" she said, looking at her hands as her fingertips vanished; the air ate the rest of her fingers and started on her arms.

Epiales, who had as of yet been concerned with Hypnos, turned to us. "Agrona!" He rushed to her side. "How could —" Epiales said, tears in his eyes. "Agrona, I will have justice for you."

"I don't think so, Epiales," Hypnos said. "This is it for you, and I won't make the same mistake again. This time, I will kill you."

"NO!" a loud voice cackled through the air. "That is enough! There has been enough gods' bloodshed this day!"

Darkness invaded the room. Even the light from the Heart of Urgu went dark. I could not see in front of my face.

CHAPTER 51

RED

"Nox?" I whispered. She was the only one who could make darkness like this, so total and complete that I couldn't see the nose on my face.

"Yes, my child," Nox replied. "All my children. This has gone on long enough. I thought you could be adults, but I see that was naïve."

"He started it," Hypnos replied, mumbling.

"And I am ending it," Nox roared. "I thought you could come to terms on your own without violence. I thought Erebus would show you that death was not the way, but he failed me, and you."

"It's not his fault your son is a prick," Queen Aine said.

"Am not!" Epiales said. "Mom!"

The wind in the room shifted to Epiales. "And you. How dare you rampage over my kingdom when I gave you a perfectly good one to rule."

"Good?" he screamed. "It was filled with monsters!"

"You love monsters, doll." Nox's voice was calm and caring. "You told me yourself every day of your childhood."

"That was ages ago!" Epiales said. "So, because I used

to like monsters, you cast me out with them, as you stayed here with your favorite son?"

"Hardly my favorite, my love," Nox said.

"Hey!" Hypnos shouted.

"I love you both," she said with a sigh. "All my children. But you are all wholly disappointing."

"What does that mean?" Epiales said.

The voice got softer. "It means it's time for you to come with me, my dear."

"I'm not a child."

"Then learn to act like an adult! Until then, you will come with me and help me rebuild the Dream Realm."

"And what of me?" Hypnos said.

"You can stay as well. We will all three rule this realm together, like a family."

"And what of the Nightmare Realm?" I asked, immediately regretting it.

I felt the wind shift to me. "I have that under control. I am not some third-rate god, my child."

"I can't rule with him next to me," Hypnos said.

"Then you can leave," Nox said in a matter-of-fact tone. "And make your life among the clouds, but this is over. I was a fool to think that either of you could rule a land by yourself. You are selfish and impetuous. I suppose we all are, frankly."

"Why didn't you come before?" Rose asked.

"I watched this place slide downhill over the generations, but I thought it was my job as its creator to let it find its equilibrium. I never thought that would lead to such chaos. Now, come, child."

"What about me?" Hypnos said.

"I need some time with your brother alone. When you are ready, you know where to find me."

The darkness enveloped Epiales and imploded upon itself. It was over, or at least I thought it was. I didn't know what the next thing would be, but I felt a great sense of relief. The weight in my chest lifted, the one that had been with me since the moment the dreams left Urgu. Maybe, I thought to myself, just maybe, my job was done.

It is not done, my child. It has only just begun. Nox's voice whispered to me. *Remember, you are my charge now, and I expect you to fulfill our bargain.*

CHAPTER 52
NIMUE

Once the orderlies realized we were trying to save Brad, not kill him, they released us from custody. I left Gwen and her beau to their joy and walked toward the entrance of the hospital.

As I walked out the front door, the glass in front of me slid open. I was stunned by this beautiful bit of magic. Somebody once told me that technology, when advanced enough, was indistinguishable from magic. This world seemed full of magic, and I couldn't wait to explore it.

For the first time in a long time, I felt true joy in my heart. In the Dream Realm, every emotion was dull and muted, but here I felt the full force of happiness. I was free to do anything I wanted, at least until Etsop called me again. I would deal with that when it came. In the meantime, I was free to build a life for myself in this strange new world.

"Hey!" I heard Gwen shout behind me. "Where are you going?"

I smiled at her when I turned around. "I was giving you space. After all, you and Brad have a lot to catch up on."

She smiled. "I appreciate that, but...where will you go?"

"I don't know, and I'm okay with that. I want to eat everything I can get my hands on and smell every smell I can find."

"You're going to get very fat, then."

"That sounds lovely, frankly."

Gwen put her hands in her pockets. "At least let me give you a ride into town. We're in the middle of nowhere."

"I don't mind the walk."

"You will, trust me. I don't know what it was like in the Dream Realm, but here, the sun is very hot, and you'll die if you walk under it for too long."

I squinted up at the sky. She had a point. "Very well, I accept."

"Good," Gwen said. "Now, they're testing Brad for the next couple of days before they discharge him, but they think they can release him this week. I'd...like it if you stayed and helped me with him, at least until he's back on his feet."

"Like a nurse?"

"Kind of, if you want to call it that. I mean, I still have to work, assuming I still have a job, and I figure the two of you have both been out of it for long enough that it will be fun to watch you learn things together."

I shook my head. "I don't want to impose."

She grabbed my hands and pulled me close. "It's not an imposition. You're the only reason I got my boyfriend back. The last thing you are in an imposition."

The last friend I had, I killed. This one, I would fight like hell to keep, and make sure nothing bad ever happened to her. "Okay."

"Great," she said, wrapping her arms under mine. "Where to first?"

"How about breakfast?"

"Sounds perfect."

CHAPTER 53
RED

I was bandaging Balor's arm beside the Heart of Urgu when Rose walked up to me. I had seen her milling around in the background, too timid to approach me, while Hypnos paced the floor addressing his subjects. It warmed my heart when she plucked up the courage to approach me.

"Hi," she said.

The truth was, I had no great desire to see her. After all, I was the reason she was dead. The guilt ate at me. I should have known that the whole of the nobility would turn on her, and yet, I let them kill her.

"Hello," I said, standing. Balor rolled over and tried to sleep. "It is good to see you are alive."

She nodded. "You too."

I choked back my disappointment in myself. "I'm very sorry that I couldn't protect you, my queen."

Rose held up her hand. "You couldn't have known. Nobody could have known."

"I have felt shame since it happened."

She smiled. "I absolve you from that shame." She gestured around us. "Look at what you have done here. You helped us save the Dream Realm. We should be thanking you."

I felt myself flush. "It was my pleasure." I paused, reminded of my bargain with Nox. I had to fulfill my end of it. "I do have a request for Hypnos, if you would do me the honor of introducing me."

"Of course," she said, walking up to the sparkling pink god of dreams. "Hypnos, I would like to introduce you to a friend of mine."

Hypnos turned toward us and smiled. "Of course. Any friend of Rose's is a friend of mine."

"This is—Well, I call her Red."

"Gabrielle," I said, shaking Hypnos's outstretched hand.

"I'll leave you to it," Rose said. She hesitated for a moment, looking down at her hands, then up at me. "Before I go, though, do you have any idea what happened to Chelle?"

I shook my head. "I'm sorry, the last time I saw her she was bringing your ashes to the Spindle and was very much alive. I expected her to find her here, actually."

She nodded. "Thank you."

When she had walked away, Hypnos crossed his arms. "You have something to ask me."

"I do, your majesty. I have lived in the Dream Realm for eons and have served enough lives. I wish to return to Earth, as Nimue did, and live out the rest of my life in service to myself."

"Are you sure?" Hypnos said, his eyebrows raised. "It's quite different out there than you remember."

I nodded. *I have no choice.* "I'm sure that it is, but I have my orde—I have made up my mind."

"That is a big request," Hypnos said. "Do you understand that the only way to reenter the world is through the consciousness of another, effectively stealing their body?"

I blinked. "I did not. I was to— I don't wa—"

He held up his hand. "I'm just kidding. That's something that demons say to trick people, and because they lack the power of the gods."

He touched my shoulder, and a wave of heat rippled through me. I cocked back my head and smelled the world for the first time in a long time. When I looked down at my hands, I felt blood beating through them.

"What did you do?"

"I infused you with a bit of my essence, like I did with Rose. I don't have much to give, but it corporealized your soul." He turned and pointed to the glowing white door behind the Heart of Urgu. "When you walk out that door, you will be back on Earth, and all the good and bad that comes with it. If you would be so kind as to wait outside for me, I will bring you off the mountain. I have to find out if Rose is coming with me or not."

"Thank you."

I was going back to Earth.

Truly, and for the first time in a long time, a wave of joy rushed over me, all the way down to my soul. I was still in service to the goddess of the night, but until she called upon me, I could build a life for myself in the strange world I had once heard of in Rose's stories.

CHAPTER 54
AINE

"I am glad you survived," Rose said to me as she turned from Hypnos and Red. "Although, I should have assumed. You have a way of surviving."

"I watched gods ripped asunder in front of me," I replied. "And all of my people destroyed, but yes, somehow I survived."

Rose looked around nervously and gulped. "Not to be indelicate about your loss, but have you seen Chelle?" she asked.

I couldn't tell her, so I just shook my head. "Not since—you should ask the Fates." I pointed to Clotho, who was standing next to us.

"Hello, my child." Clotho cleared her throat. "Your soul is so familiar. Are you the Dreamer girl whose soul fell to ash?"

Rose nodded. "I am."

"It is good to see you reconstituted," Lachesis said, walking closer to us. "We worried about you, but it all worked out."

"You...are the Fates, then?"

They both nodded, before Clotho stepped forward from the Heart of Urgu. "So was your love, Chelle. She talked of you often."

"You knew Chelle?" Rose said, almost jumping.

Lachesis nodded. "We did. She became the third Fate to replace our fallen Atropos."

"What happened to her?" Rose said. "I've been looking for her everywhere."

Clotho sighed and turned to the Heart of Urgu. "She gave her life to restart the Heart and save us all."

Rose's knees knocked together and tears filled her eyes. "No. No. It's not possible—"

"I'm afraid it is," Lachesis said, placing a hand on the girl's shoulder. "She was brave, braver than most, possibly all of us. You are only here, the world is only here, because of her. We owe everything to her."

Rose dropped to the ground, unable to speak. Clotho bent down to comfort her. I went to do the same, but Lachesis cupped me in her hands. "Let Clotho console her. She is better at it than we are."

"She is my friend."

"Then you want her comforted by one who will hear her the best. Besides, I need to speak with you."

"What do you want of me?"

Lachesis set me down beside her and stared at me for a long time before saying, "I want to know what you will do now."

"Shouldn't you know? You are a Fate, after all."

She shook her head. "I am blind to your path forward. You could stay here, or—well, let's just say you have many options before you, but I don't want to say too much."

"Urgu is my home," I said. "There will be more fairies traveling to this place now that the Heart has restarted.

Somebody must stay to lead this realm, and my people again, and make sure nothing like Epiales ever comes again."

"A wise decision, and one I doubt you would have made in the past."

"When I was younger, I was stupid and brash. Perhaps I will think the same of myself in a year's time, but right now, duty is the most important thing. I have a duty to guide my people here in Urgu, so...that's what I'm going to do."

It was a bitter pill to swallow, but it was the truth. I could be happy here, as long as I showed my people how to live, and how to lead.

CHAPTER 55

ROSE

I couldn't bear the thought of losing Chelle in the Dream Realm, of not being able to say goodbye to her. Of not being able to hold her in my arms again.

I had to get out of there. I pushed through the refugees and through the door back to Earth. When I got there, my chest heaved and I cried until I had no tears left, and then I collapsed and cried some more, screaming into the dirt and rocks outside the Obsidian Spindle.

When I finally couldn't cry for another second, I heard soft steps coming toward me. "Don't."

"I'm sorry," Hypnos said, kneeling next to me. "I know how much she meant to you, and now, how much she means to all of Urgu."

"Did you know?" I said, turning to him. "Did you know she was dead?"

"I can feel souls returning, but I can't feel any specific one." He pressed his hand to his forehead. "Speaking of."

He closed his eyes and a jolt of energy pulsated through me. "What was that?"

"I rescinded my claim to your soul. It would have come

to me when you died, but now, you are free. Don't be so willing to give it away next time. Most gods are not so forgiving, but you have done me a great service. I could never ask you to come back to the Dream Realm while your love still rests out among the stars."

I sat up and wiped the dirt and tears off my face. "What do you mean? Chelle is dead, you said so yourself."

Hypnos sat down across from me. "Funny thing about the afterlife. Nothing is ever gone. Not really. You just have to know where to look."

I gasped. "You mean Chelle might be alive."

"In a manner of speaking." He nodded. "I don't know where to find her, but I know where I would look first."

"Where?"

He placed his shades on his face and looked directly at the sun. After a few seconds, he pinched the sides of it and a golden coin fell into his hands. "Careful, it might be hot."

He handed it to me, and he was right, it was warm in my hands, though not scalding. "What is this for?"

"Passage. Anywhere the gods roam, in any realm, as long as you have that coin and my blessing, it will grant you passage."

"Your blessing. Don't you need it for the next queen?"

Hypnos shook his head. "I think it's time we changed things up a bit. Perhaps install democracy...of a fashion."

I smiled. "Aine would make a very fine president."

"I agree," Hypnos said with a chuckle. "Between her, Epiales, my mother, and myself, I think we will be okay. Perhaps we'll even get television. That's what I'll miss most of all."

"Will I ever see you again?"

Hypnos closed my hand around the coin and then

placed his hands around mine. "Anytime you need to see me, you know how to get here."

"Thank you." I pushed myself up to standing. "You never told me where to look, though. For Chelle, I mean."

He stood up next to me. "In a small town in Turkey called Pamukkale. There is a gate to the underworld there. You can ask Hades personally whether he has seen your paramour."

"Thank you."

"He is always in a foul mood until his beloved returns in the spring, so I would wait for a couple of months for him to come around."

"I'm not sure I can do that," I said. "But I'll try."

"I can't believe it," I heard from behind me. I turned to see Red standing in front of the door to the Dream Realm, tears swelling in her eyes. She looked at her hands like she was certain they would dissolve. She smiled broadly. "I didn't think that was possible. Your boss is very powerful."

"Not boss," Hypnos said. "Just a friend." He looked over at Red. "I know I told you that I would bring you down the mountain, but I realized that somebody must take the key back and protect it. I would very much like it to be you."

"I would be honored," Red said. "But how will we get home?"

Hypnos pulled a dream orb out of his pocket. "When I am gone and you have the key, smash this onto the ground and tell it where you want to go." He turned to me. "And as for you. Do you remember the casino in Reno?"

I nodded.

Hypnos pulled a casino chip out of his pocket. "I placed a rather sizeable bet that we would save the Dream Realm, even though the odds were against us." He placed the chip in my other hand. "I believe that's enough never to have to deal with your horrible family or healthcare system ever again."

I smiled. "Thank you."

He walked into the door and vanished. Red walked over to the door and locked it, then placed the key in a pouch around her waist.

"Are you ready to go?" Red asked, holding the orb out in front of her.

"Absolutely."

"Where are we going?"

"On an adventure."

"I love it."

You just finished *The Red Rider,* the fourth book in The Obsidian Spindle Saga. If you loved this book, please consider leaving a review on your favorite storefront. Reviews are the best way for me to see if people want me to continue a series.

Make sure to stay reading after the author note for a preview of *The Sword Wielder,* the fifth book in the Obsidian Spindle Saga.

AUTHOR NOTE

It started with a book cover. My favorite cover designer posted a pre-made cover on her website with the title "The Sleeping Beauty."

It was perfect, and I had to have it, even if I had no idea what would come from it. The entirety of the Obsidian Spindle was seeded in that cover. From that, I started designing this world in a notebook nearly three years ago, while I was writing eighteen books in eighteen months.

As I did, I thought about all the things I wanted to write about in the future, and I added it to this crazy notebook filled with characters, and maps, and mythology. Every time I took a break from another book series, I would write a little bit more in that journal. There was a bit of fairy tales, mythology, portal fantasy, romance, drama, comedy, magic, horror, and just about anything I could ever imagine writing about in my life.

I promised myself that this series would have everything I loved in it. Somehow, I figured out how to take all those things and smash it into one series, and hopefully it made sense when it was all done.

This isn't the end of the Obsidian Spindle Saga, but it's the end of the first coda. We're done in the Dream Realm, for the moment at least, and now I want to expand out and show other realms and other worlds. I can't wait to show you the underworld, other planets, and our main characters as they explore the universe together and apart, trying to save everything from falling into darkness.

I'm planning at least eight books for this series, and hopefully many, many more. Who knows, perhaps there will be even more after that, or perhaps there will be less. I am as excited for the future of this series as I am for these first four books.

I hope you loved them as much as I loved making them. I promise to keep making them as long as you keep reading them.

If you like *The Red Rider,* keep reading for a preview of the fifth book in the series, *The Sword Wielder.*

THE SWORD WIELDER PREVIEW

Book 5 of the Obsidian Spindle Saga
By:
Russell Nohelty

Edited by:
Leah Lederman

Proofread by:
Katrina Roets

Cover by:
JV Arts

Formatting by:
Turbo Kitten Industries

GWEN

"Welcome to King Arthur's Court," I said, grinning so widely and fraudulently that the sides of my cheeks throbbed. I had been on shift for ten hours and was scheduled until close for the third time this week. Most of my coworkers used Adderall to keep them up, but I did it the old-fashioned way—tons of caffeine. So much caffeine that I could barely hold a tray or refill water cups, my hands shook so much.

But it was okay. It was all okay. I was making good money at a crappy job, and I've had enough crappy jobs to know that good money didn't come easy, so I took it as a win, even if I was about to fall over from sleep deprivation.

"Can I interest you in a round table platter to start out?" I asked the family of four that had just settled down into a four topper in my section. Mama, Daddy, with two adorable children who fought over the pack of crayons I brought for them. Usually the 9 pm crowd were more sports fans who drank their weight in beer, ate our free peanuts, and tipped generously as they stumbled away, sloshed. A rather normal looking nuclear family coming in so late could only mean they were road-trippers, deliriously tired after a long day on the road, and they tipped terribly.

As the curly haired mother replied to me, a cheer erupted from the overcrowded bar and drowned out her voice. I used to think sports were stupid, but when the totality of the bar screamed in elation, it meant something good for the home team. After a big 49ers win, tips doubled for the next three days, which made me a fan.

"I'm sorry, ma'am," I replied once the cheering died down. "I didn't catch that."

She scoffed. "Maybe you should open your ears. I said that we needed a minute. We'll just take four waters in the meantime."

"I don't want water!" The little girl said, slapping her hands against her pink dress. "I want soda!"

"It's too late for that, muffin," the man said, exasperated, before looking up at me. "Sorry, we've been driving all day, and we're really hungry. I promise my family isn't usually this rude."

"Harold!" The woman screamed.

"It's okay, sir," I replied with another smile. "Your family is lovely, and I know all about traveling pains. I'll get you those waters. Meanwhile, if you need any recommendations on the menu, let me know."

I spun on my heels and took a deep breath. As I walked away, the mother muttered "she wasn't flirting with you, Harold. She was just being polite". It wouldn't be the first time that a man misread my politeness as flirtation. Heck, it wasn't even the first time in the last hour. The only solace was those types of men tended to be big tippers. I needed to remember to hand him the bill, even if the wife asked for it.

"No, we don't have that tonight," I heard Nimue

grumble from across the restaurant. "I don't know. Get off my back."

Her red hair shook as she snarled at a couple of leather-clad men sitting at a table near the front window. Her brown peasant vest wasn't buttoned, and her name tag was crooked, which were both violations of the dress code. *Why can't she just follow instructions?*

I stopped in front of the ordering screen and put in four waters for table thirty-six. I checked to see if the nachos for table 14 were ready, as they were a particularly ornery bunch, even more so than the road-tripping family that I just left.

Seeing that the nachos were done, I swung into the back and scooped it from the order window, leaving before the short order cook, Miguel, could comment about the shortness of my skirt, as if it was my preferred manner of dress and not a ridiculous contrivance of my 'wench' costume. Of course, I would never say such a thing, because then all of the good shifts would go to Andrea, or Christa, and I would be stuck with nothing but morning breakfast rush, where nobody tipped well, except on Mimosa Sunday, which was a drunken bonanza.

"Here you go," I said to two gruff looking bikers with long hair who had clearly never met an electric razor. I slid the nachos to them and then turned away. I felt one of their hands flick up the back of my skirt, and I prickled up, but I plastered a smile on my face and merely cocked my head coyly to them.

"Fresh," I cooed as I walked away.

I noticed Nimue fuming as I reached the server station. "Are you going to let them treat you that way?"

"Yeah," I said. "If I play my cards right, I'll get a 30% tip from those two jagholes."

She rolled her eyes. "You're demeaning yourself."

"Says you. I say I'm playing the role of a lifetime, and I'm cleaning up." I looked over to the two bikers and waved slowly at them. "Besides, they'll never be in here again. They're clearly just passing through."

"How do you know?" Nimue asked.

"Patches on their vest are all from Las Vegas, which I'll bet dollars to donuts is their home base. Probably just cruising through."

"Maybe they're just tacky jagholes who like buying souvenirs from places they've been and tormenting cute waitresses."

"Thank you for the compliment." I smiled, even though I knew she wasn't trying to give me one. "And if I'm wrong, then they'll give me a 30% tip next time, too, as long as I don't rock the boat."

"This is the worst job." Nimue crossed her arms across her chest. "I can't believe you willingly work here."

"I don't willingly do anything," I said. "This is the best job I can find, and when I find a better one, then I'll leave her so fast—"

"And if you never do?" Nimue asked.

"Then I'll make the best of this one until I die, I guess."

She shifted her weight to her left hip. "Being a nothing burger kind of sucks."

"What did you think it would be like?" I asked.

"I don't know. That I could just live a normal life—"

"This is a normal life." I punched into the order service and noticed that one of Nimue's orders was ready. "Table six's order is up."

"I know," she replied. "It's been there for ten minutes. I just can't deal with them."

"That's literally the job. It's probably cold now. They're going to have to make it again, and they'll dock your pay."

"They can try," she snarled.

"They don't have to try. They just will."

"This is ridiculous."

I sighed. "Look, just go home alright. I'll handle your section and split your tips. You obviously aren't in any mood to be here."

"You'd do that?" Nimue replied, surprisingly open to the idea, just like she always was.

"Sure," I replied. "I stuck my neck out for you to get this job. Remember that?"

"Yeah, I do," Nimue said, exasperated. "Do you want a medal?"

I shook my head. "No, just maybe a little gratitude."

"This job sucks, and we both know it. You should not have to risk anything, or get any reward, for helping somebody become a slave."

"Then quit." I turned to her. "It won't be the first time. Or the tenth time. Or the fif—"

"I get it," Nimue said. "You don't understand. I was a queen in Oz. I was waited on hand and foot, not the other way around. This is so demeaning."

"This is my life." I stared into her eyes. "And it's your life too, your highness."

She realized she crossed a line. "I'm sorry. I will do better tomorrow. I promise."

"Just go, alright." I turned into the order window and scooped up her table's order. "I can't look at you right now."

ROSE

What happens when supply outstrips demand in a free market society?

Ugh. I couldn't care less.

Focus, Rose, this was the last question on your last exam of the semester, and then you were free for the whole summer. A whole summer of sneaking into the underworld to find Chelle.

No, it wasn't a traditional summer, and I wouldn't be writing a report on it for homeroom next year—also, they didn't do that in college, thank the gods. I was so excited that I could barely sit in my seat...but I had to. I already missed one semester of school in a coma, and I couldn't risk flunking out. By the time I got Chelle back, she would be at least a year behind, which meant I needed to finish school, get a job, and support her as she learned to be human again.

That's funny.

Chelle wasn't really human, was she? At least, not completely. However, it's a little harder to say she had to learn how to half-gorgon/half-human again, even though that was technically correct, which is the best form of correct, it didn't roll off the tongue quite as nicely.

Mmmm...tongue. I could still taste Chelle on my lips, even though she had been going for over a year. I couldn't wait to—

"Five minutes!" The proctor shouted from the front of the room. I took a quick peek around and saw there were only ten students left in the once packed lecture hall. Crud.

Alright...*what happens when supply outstrips demand in a free market society?*

Ugh, come on Rose, you know this. You studied for this so hard and even though most of those hours were trying not to fall asleep, you should have at least learned this by osmosis falling asleep on top of the textbook.

I pressed my mechanical pencil down on the paper so hard that the lead snapped. I clicked another piece of lead out and stared at the paper. In a rush all my sleep deprived studying hit me.

Prices will lower until it hits equilibrium with demand. This is the law of demand.

Was that right? I willed myself to care, to search my memory until I was sure that was the right answer. I skimmed through the exam for errors, but there was no chance I had the energy to make sure my answers were right. As long as I got a C or better, I would never have to take economics again for my whole life.

I stood up and took a big stretch. I didn't bother to change out of my pink sweats before the exam, and looking around most of the other students made similar fashion choices. The joys of college. Nobody gave a frigging heck about how they looked.

I placed my paper on the top of the stack and smiled at the pimply proctor, noticing a thick layer of gunk that caked onto the edges of his thick glasses. He had been the bane of my existence all semester, and now I was free of him and his greasy face.

"Have a great summer," I said to him, lightly.

"You too," he replied with a smug smirk. He loved this school so much, and it showed through on every inch of him. *Easy killer. You're not at Yale. Take your pride down a few pegs.* "Hope you don't die."

I nearly skipped out of the room. If I had any of my magic left, I would have floated on a cloud, but I didn't. I had left it all in the Dream Realm. I pulled open the door to the room and saw Jamil sitting on the stoop across from the door. When she saw me, she waved.

"Hey!" She shouted.

"Hi?" I replied, furrowing my brow. "Were you waiting for me?"

We had grown close since saving the Dream Realm. Even though she totally abandoned Hypnos and I in Reno, I didn't hold it against her...too much. She pressed the red amulet necklace she wore against her neck as she stood. The amulet created an illusion that allowed her to present herself as a brown-skinned Indian woman instead of a wood nymph with skin like bark. The only thing about her illusion that wasn't a lie were the big, brown eyes that held a thousand secrets behind them.

"Of course I was." Jamil said, hopping off the ledge toward me. "It's the last class of the semester. You're done. I'm done. I thought we could get lunch and tell this school it can suck butt."

"That would sound lovely, if I didn't know why you wanted to have lunch with me."

"Ulterior motives?" She pressed her hand against her chest and feigned offense. "Moi? I'm hurt."

I picked up my pace as I walked past her. "You have until I get to the car to speak your peace, and if you tell me the truth, maybe I'll have lunch with you."

"Oh, the great and powerful Rose will come down from her high horse to slum it with the rest of us?" She rolled her eyes. "What an honor."

I spun to her, stopping my gait. "That's funny, especially since I was the queen of Oz."

"Yeah, for like five seconds."

"Only officially!" I shouted, before lowering my voice. "I was like, unofficially, the queen for a month. Will you please just spit it out, already."

"Fine!" Jamil growled. "I know you're going to the Underworld to find Chelle, and I know you think it's a good idea, but it's really a stupid idea. I had to tell you one more time before you got yourself killed."

"Noted," I said with my fakest smile. "Is that it?"

"No," Jamil said, trying to land her next thought. "She's dead, Rose. You can't just bring the dead back from being dead."

"Gabrielle was dead once, too, and look at her. She's kind of sort of normal." Red had escaped the Dream Realm and joined me on Earth. With the money Hypnos gave me, I rented us both an apartment. Once I got Chelle back, she was going to have to find a new place, but for now, it was nice to have company in the large apartment we shared. "Why can't Chelle come back? You know as well as me magic is as powerful as it is stupid. So who knows the rules, really?"

"First, Red is not all there, and you know it. She's completely clueless about anything and everything."

"That's just because she's like ancient. Chelle isn't from

some ancient version of Earth. She'll be fine if she comes back. It will be just like old times."

"Nothing will be like old times. There's no going back." Jamil sighed. "It's not healthy, Rose. You'll never get over her if—"

"I don't want to get over her. I want her back." I bit my lip, trying to contain my anger. "Your objection is noted, now piss off."

I started to walk away from her, but she caught up and pulled my arm toward her. "Wait."

I broke free of her grasp. "What?"

"I don't want to leave angry." She grabbed me and pulled me tight. "I love you, even though you're an idiot."

I squeeze her tightly. "I love you, too."

After a long moment she released me. "Please can we have lunch? I promise we'll just talk about stupid stuff, no Chelle. I'm buying."

I chuckled. "That's funny. You're broke as a joke. I'm buying."

"Phew," she said, wrapping her arm around me. "I was hoping you would say that."

If you liked that preview, then be on the lookout for *The Sword Wielder, coming* in 2022.

ALSO BY RUSSELL NOHELTY

The Obsidian Spindle Saga

The Godsverse Chronicles

Ichabod Jones: Monster Hunter

Cthulhu is Hard to Spell

My Father Didn't Kill Himself

Sorry for Existing

Gumshoes: The Case of Madison's Father

The Invasion Saga

The Vessel

Worst Thing in the Universe

The Void Calls Us Home

The Marked Ones

The Little Bird and the Little Worm

Gherkin Boy

Find a complete list at

https://www.russellnohelty.com/books/

About the Author

Russell Nohelty is a USA Today bestselling author, publisher, and speaker. He is the author of dozens of novels and graphic novels including The Godsverse Chronicles, The Obsidian Spindle Saga, and Ichabad Jones: Monster Hunter. He has a very entertaining newsletter, which you can join at www.russellnohelty.com. He lives in Los Angeles with his wife and dogs.

Get one of my favorite books for free at:
www.russellnohelty.com/mail
Substack:
https://authorstack.substack.com
Bookbub:
https://www.bookbub.com/profile/russell-nohelty